Praise for the Novels a
   Finalist for the *Los Angeles Times* Book Prize

"A keen voice, profound insight . . . devilishly entertaining."   —*Los Angeles Times*

"Goldberg's prose is deceptively smooth, like a vanilla milk shake spiked with grain alcohol."
                                                —*Chicago Tribune*

"[A] creepy, strangely sardonic, definitely disturbing version of Middle America . . . and that, of course, is where the fun begins."   —*LA Weekly*

"Perfect . . . with all the sleaze and glamour of the old paperbacks of fifty years ago." —*Kirkus Reviews*

"Striking and affecting. . . . Goldberg is a gifted writer, poetic and rigorous . . . a fiction tour de force . . . a haunting book."   —*January Magazine*

Praise for the Series

"Likably lighthearted and cool as a smart-mouthed loner . . . cheerfully insouciant."
                                             —*The New York Times*

"Brisk and witty."   —*The Christian Science Monitor*

"[A] swell new spy series . . . highly enjoyable."
                                                —*Chicago Tribune*

continued . . .

"Violence, babes, and a cool guy spy . . . slick and funny and a lotta fun." —*New York Post*

"Smart, charmingly irreverent . . . pleasantly warped." —*Detroit Free Press*

"Snazzy." —*Entertainment Weekly*

"Terrifically entertaining . . . neat and crisp as citrus soda." —*Seattle Post-Intelligencer*

"Breezy cloak-and-dagger ingenuity. [A] nicely pitched action-comedy hero: handsome, smart, neurotic, tough, funny, sensitive . . . Michael Westen is Jim Rockford and MacGyver filtered through Carl Hiassen. Entertaining, in other words." —*LA Weekly*

burn notice
The Fix

TOD GOLDBERG

Based on the USA Network Television Series
Created by Matt Nix

AN OBSIDIAN MYSTERY

OBSIDIAN
Published by New American Library, a division of
Penguin Group (USA) Inc., 375 Hudson Street,
New York, New York 10014, USA
Penguin Group (Canada), 90 Eglinton Avenue East, Suite 700, Toronto,
Ontario M4P 2Y3, Canada (a division of Pearson Penguin Canada Inc.)
Penguin Books Ltd., 80 Strand, London WC2R 0RL, England
Penguin Ireland, 25 St. Stephen's Green, Dublin 2,
Ireland (a division of Penguin Books Ltd.)
Penguin Group (Australia), 250 Camberwell Road, Camberwell, Victoria 3124,
Australia (a division of Pearson Australia Group Pty. Ltd.)
Penguin Books India Pvt. Ltd., 11 Community Centre, Panchsheel Park,
New Delhi - 110 017, India
Penguin Group (NZ), 67 Apollo Drive, Rosedale, North Shore 0632,
New Zealand (a division of Pearson New Zealand Ltd.)
Penguin Books (South Africa) (Pty.) Ltd., 24 Sturdee Avenue,
Rosebank, Johannesburg 2196, South Africa

Penguin Books Ltd., Registered Offices:
80 Strand, London WC2R 0RL, England

First published by Obsidian, an imprint of New American Library,
a division of Penguin Group (USA) Inc.

First Printing, August 2008
10 9 8 7 6 5 4 3 2

TM & © 2008 Twentieth Century Fox Film Corporation. All Rights Reserved.

OBSIDIAN and logo are trademarks of Penguin Group (USA) Inc.

Printed in the United States of America

Without limiting the rights under copyright reserved above, no part of this
publication may be reproduced, stored in or introduced into a retrieval
system, or transmitted, in any form, or by any means (electronic, mechanical,
photocopying, recording, or otherwise), without the prior written permission of both the copyright owner and the above publisher of this book.

PUBLISHER'S NOTE
This is a work of fiction. Names, characters, places, and incidents either are
the product of the author's imagination or are used fictitiously, and any
resemblance to actual persons, living or dead, business establishments,
events, or locales is entirely coincidental.
    The publisher does not have any control over and does not assume any
responsibility for author or third-party Web sites or their content.

If you purchased this book without a cover you should be aware that this
book is stolen property. It was reported as "unsold and destroyed" to the
publisher and neither the author nor the publisher has received any payment for this "stripped book."

The scanning, uploading, and distribution of this book via the Internet or
via any other means without the permission of the publisher is illegal and
punishable by law. Please purchase only authorized electronic editions, and
do not participate in or encourage electronic piracy of copyrighted materials.
Your support of the author's rights is appreciated.

For Wendy, for trying to stay up on the latest nights, and never complaining when they became the earliest mornings.

ACKNOWLEDGMENTS

I am ever grateful to Matt Nix for lending me his creation for a few hundred pages and for his unwavering confidence in my ability to bring Michael Westen to the page. And to Todd Harris, who told us both about ten years ago that we should work together. Some things just take time.

My thanks to my brother, Lee Goldberg, for the midnight e-mail that got this started, and for the continuing midnight e-mails to make sure I was awake and writing. My agent, Jennie Dunham, for her wise counsel, smart reading and driving up to Vermont in the dead of winter to, I suspect, also make sure I was writing. Kristen Weber, my editor, for giving me the time to do it right, and for understanding when I still needed more time.

Much thanks are also due to: Brenda Holcomb, for tending and feeding two writers on deadline at the same time; my sisters, the wonderful authors Linda Woods and Karen Dinino, for being part of this odd journey we've all hitched ourselves to; my ever-patient students at both the UCLA Extension Writers' Program and in the MFA program at UC–Riverside, who received many papers days and weeks late while this was being written; and of course my wife, Wendy, who lives through every word.

Since I'm not actually a spy, I'm happy to report that nothing in this book will guide you toward actually blowing anything up (nor, likewise, defusing any bombs). I found several sources very helpful, however, particularly *The Spycraft Manual* by Barry Davies; the compendium of terribly frightening and eminently enlightening (though not in a good way) mortgage-fraud cases found on mortgagefraudblog. com; *The Tao of Spycraft: Intelligence Theory and Practice in Traditional China* by Ralph D. Sawyer; *The Anarchist Cookbook* by William Powell; *On Killing: The Psychological Cost of Learning to Kill in War and Society* by Dave Grossman . . . and a well-timed e-mail from Michael Wilson.

1

When you're a spy, certain things come easy. You never have to pay your parking tickets. The IRS leaves you pretty much alone provided you don't try to deduct TEC-9s from your 1040EZ. It's okay if you have sex with someone you don't actually like. In fact it's often encouraged, and if on the off chance you fall in love with the wrong person and have to kill them, or they try to kill you, your boss rarely asks for you to fill out a purchase order for a body bag or extra bullets.

But not even being a spy gets you out of having lunch with your mother.

It was a Tuesday, and because she lied and told me I was taking her to the orthopedist, I was sitting poolside at the Hotel Oro having lunch with my mother, Madeline. The Hotel Oro is one of those hotels on South Beach that no one actually stays at, but everyone seems to visit. It has an Olympic-sized infinity pool, which seems odd when you consider the ocean is only five yards away, but then the ocean doesn't have full bar service and cocktail girls dressed in gold bikinis serving you finger foods. At night, DJs spin Eurotrash for Paris Hilton and the entire hotel throbs onto the street, like it's an actual living creature that feeds on celebrities. My mother kept lifting her sunglasses up to stare at the people being seated at the tables around us.

"You expecting someone?" I asked.

"Fiona said she might join us," my mother said.

Fiona was my girlfriend for a while. Then she was not my girlfriend for a while. Then it was just confusing, and a little violent, in a good way, and now she's more like a business partner, but might be my girlfriend again sometime soon. It's complicated. "I don't like you calling her," I said.

"She told me the cutest thing yesterday," she said.

The problem with having your business partner being your former and maybe future girlfriend is that it's hard to make any essential mandates about behavior. You risk pissing off someone who may or may not call your mother either way. It's only slightly worse when the same person happens to be a former IRA gunrunner who still has something of an opaque moral center and who doesn't understand personal boundaries.

"Do tell," I said.

"Just girl stuff, Michael."

Girl stuff. Ten years of interrogating hostile enemy targets, you'd think I'd be able to break through that code, but give me twenty Enigma machines and fifty men sitting in a locked room at Quantico, and there'd be no way of figuring out what the hell *girl stuff* means.

I'd have been more upset with this whole line of conversation had I not been distracted, which is actually how I generally like to feel during conversations with my mother. That way I don't get too emotionally involved, or, in a pinch, can plead ignorance if important dates or activities are mentioned.

Across the pool, three white guys in Cuban shirts, tan chinos and ankle holsters were trying their best to look natural, which would have been easier if they weren't all wearing the same shirt, which is what happens when you try to look natural by letting some intern buy your resort wear. That they weren't trying to look natural while monitoring me was of some concern.

"We should do this more often, Michael," my mother said.

"What's *this*, exactly?"

"Family time. You know it wouldn't kill you to take me out to lunch every week. I read where the president calls his mother every day. She even vacations with him sometimes."

The three white guys in Cubans were a little on the chunky side and their skin was almost translucent, which meant they weren't normally field agents. Field agents tend to have a few fast twitch muscles and maybe a decent farmer's tan from sitting with their arms out car windows, waiting for something to happen, or snapping photos, or shooting at moving targets. Doughy is no way to go through life. Everything works less effectively when you've got plaque in your arteries, but doughy also says: Happy. Content. Secure.

Miami-Dad's finest: The Strategic Investigations Bureau.

SIB agents are paper hounds and numbers guys. Loophole chasers. Get them outside and maybe they know how to handle a gun, but you take them out of their comfort zone, you put a knife to their throat or you show them a little of their own blood, and they turn into hand puppets.

"That's great," I said. "Next time I see the president, I'll let him know you're free."

"I'm serious, Michael," she said. "Since you've been back, you haven't taken me to a single movie. Would it kill you take me to see a movie?"

It might. But at the moment, I was more concerned by the SIB agents. If they were anchoring the back door, that meant someone was in the front and that there was probably a gun or two aimed in this direction from one of the adjoining buildings. Most likely, the ATF was near, too.

"Ma," I said, "how did you hear about this place?"

"Fiona said we should meet here."

"When?"

"This morning. Why, Michael?"

"Did you call her?"

"Michael, I know you want your privacy, but it's not wrong for a mother to call her son's girlfriend.

Do you know when I was dating your father that your grandmother used to call me every morning?"

If you're a tourist, one of the best things about coming to South Beach is the ease with which you can pool hop from one hotel to the next. Why, you could rappel down from the Hotel Victor's rooftop pool directly into the Hotel Oro's if you happened to have that skill set, which, judging by the two slightly more athletic-looking agents poised to do just that very thing across the way, they're now teaching younger and more agile government recruits. Though I suspected the ones at the Victor *were* actually ATF.

"I didn't know that," I said. I stood up as casually as possible, so as not to arouse any suspicion in the SIB or ATF agents. Mistakes get made when you haven't been out of the office for a few years and now have a license to shoot someone; it's doubly bad if you've been gorging on fatty foods in the interim and are now a little nervous, are thinking, Yeah, maybe if I put a bullet into someone, like a former IRA gunrunner wanted by an alphabet soup of organizations alive or dead. Thinking, Maybe I'll get a bump. Thinking, Maybe I'll get a corner office. "Why don't we talk about it in the car?"

"But our food hasn't even arrived," Mom said.

I clenched my teeth into a polite smile, just in case I was on a camera somewhere. "We need to go," I said. "Now."

"What about Fiona?"

"Fiona won't be showing up," I said.

*   *   *

For the last ten years, I've lived wherever the government has told me to live. There were also times when I didn't live anywhere at all. Times when a helicopter would drop me in front of a target, I'd do my job, and the helicopter would pick me back up five minutes, or five hours, or five days later, depending upon the circumstances of the job and whatever collateral damage might have ensued.

You don't ask a lot of questions. You're given your assignment and you do it or you risk the consequences. My last official job as a covert operative was in the lovely city of Warri, Nigeria, vacation hotspot for large arms dealers, exhausted genocidal maniacs and anyone who loves to fall asleep to the peaceful drumming of AKs being fired into the sky.

I was sent there to dispose of a problem: A gangster was causing problems along a lucrative oil field—as in, he periodically had his people blow up the refinery, sabotage the pipeline, kill the security detail, that sort of thing—and I was there with a very simple offer of $750,000 to find some other way to entertain himself.

Sometimes, it's just easier to pay off the bad guys. Fewer bodies. Less psychic turmoil. But mostly, fewer bodies.

Everything was going swimmingly. We had a charming room in the lovely Warri Grand Hotel, where every low-level thug is treated like a higher-level thug. I didn't trust the gangster. He didn't trust me. But there was money from the American government in between us, and we both trusted *that*. The problem was that at some point between me stepping off a plane in Nigeria with the authorization to wire money into the Russian's account, and the exact moment I made the call to start the transfer, I lost my job.

If I worked at Kinko's, that wouldn't be much of a problem. I'd just strip off my name tag and walk out the door, because even on your worst day, it's unlikely a gangster will kill you if you lose your job at Kinko's. But when your job is to deliver $750,000 to a gangster and you have to try to explain to him that, unfortunately, you've just been informed that there's a burn notice on your file and therefore all pending deals you're a part of are now canceled, well, there're going to be hard feelings.

There were.

Thing is, you can't just tell a gangster that you've lost all of your security clearances, that your cover is gone, that your bank accounts have been frozen and that, for all intents and purposes, Michael Westen is pretty much just a regular guy now and he'll have to find someone else to deal with if he hopes to get his money. Even if it's the truth. Which it was. But when you get a burn notice it's not just your job you lose, it's all the fringe benefits, too.

Like assault teams.

Exit strategies.

Someone who might claim your desecrated corpse.

Thus, if you happen to get your burn notice in a place where you're likely to catch fire, too, you're obliged to figure out a more serviceable truth if continuing to breathe is a priority in your life.

Or, failing that, you fight your way out and hope to survive.

I did a combination of both, the result being that I got out of the hotel alive, barely, boarded a plane with half a rack of broken ribs, a concussion, a few chips, a few dings, passed out and woke up in Miami.

My childhood home.

The very place I ran from when I joined the military out of high school.

The place I've avoided returning to every year since.

The place where my mother, Madeline, lives in a periodic state of hypochondrial distress; where my brother, Nate, gambles and grifts; where my father is buried, but where his ghost still wanders around.

The place where I now live in a vacant loft above a nightclub. From the two windows in my loft I can see a sign store and the Little River, which winds from the coast back into the heart of the Everglades. There are exactly nine palm trees on my street. At night, after the nightclub closes, it's always exciting to watch drunks alternately piss on the palm trees or attempt to have sex against them. No one ever comes to clean them up, either way. A drug dealer named Sugar used to live beneath me until I shot him. It's the kind of neighborhood where anyone with a gun would feel right at home, but it's not anyplace I want to live.

Since finding myself in Miami, I've tried to unravel

the truth behind my burn notice. What I know: If the government truly wanted me dead, I'd be dead. They might be willing to let someone else kill me if it should happen during the daily course of life, but they aren't sending assassins to my house. That my dossier is filled with flagrant inaccuracies is of no matter, apparently. The message they've sent through various means is clear: If I want to live, I am to stay in Miami, which is why I knew the SIB and ATF agents weren't looking for me at the Hotel Oro.

Fiona, on the other hand . . .

"I had a meeting planned with a lovely new client," Fiona said. We were standing in my kitchen, and since I'd missed lunch entirely, I was trying to eat enough yogurt to raise my blood sugar to a level where I could hold a conversation with Fi without having the veins in my neck break through the skin. Plus, Fiona was wearing a yellow sundress, and when she moved, different parts of her body seemed to glow beneath the fabric, and she smelled vaguely of vanilla and strawberries. Difficult circumstances, all. "I thought I'd drop off my small package for her and then join you two poolside."

"What did you have in that package?"

"Three QBZ87s," she said.

"Three?"

"Well, more like ten," she said.

"Ten Chinese assault rifles," I said. "You just had those in your closet?"

"I stumbled on a few," she said.

When I first met Fiona, she was mostly robbing

banks and dealing arms for the IRA, but then other organizations heard about her particular abilities, and so she opted to hang a freelance shingle out in the world. When I woke up in Miami, she was sitting beside me in a hotel room, which is what happens when you forget to change your emergency contact information. I hadn't seen her since a rather hasty departure from Dublin. Interpersonal relationships have never been my strong suit.

"That's hardly enough to bring out the cavalry," I said.

"I also had a few Spear hollow points that I was providing as a service."

And this is where it always gets interesting with Fiona. "A few?"

"A case. A very small case."

"Fi."

"It was an excellent deal, Michael," she said.

"So ten Chinese assault rifles and a very small case of hollow points. That was it."

"Closer to a *gross* of hollow point *clips*, if you're going to split hairs about things."

It's never as simple as black-and-white with Fiona. While I'm virtually imprisoned in Miami, Fiona is here by choice, the only thing holding her to this place being whatever it is we have, which at the moment is strictly business . . . though, not always platonic. Like I said before: It get's complicated. That she was sitting in my loft flipping through a magazine when I returned from our aborted lunch didn't surprise me in the least. I was frankly surprised she wasn't in the backseat of my Charger when we stepped out of the hotel.

"You didn't think to maybe pick up the phone and warn me when you realized the deal was off?"

"And let you grow complacent in your job?"

In order to make money, in order to survive long enough to find out who had burned me and why, I've been forced to take a few odd jobs helping people, and Fi has been kind enough to provide tactical support. On her off days, she's got her own business interests, the less that possibly involve me and my mother in the firing line of crooked fingered agents the better.

"I was there with my *mother*."

"Who you should call more often," she said.

"You're changing the subject," I said.

Fiona stepped around me and opened up my refrigerator and stared inside. "Do you have anything with protein?"

"The point here is that you were set up, Fiona," I said.

"There's no devaluing your ability to notice the obvious," she said absently. She was pulling out old food from my refrigerator and systematically smelling items and then immediately throwing them away.

"What do you intend to do?"

Fiona finally found an apple that met her approval, bit into it and then chewed thoughtfully. "Well," she said, swallowing, "I could blow up the hotel."

"Do you even know who the buyer was?" I asked.

Fiona waved me off. "No one who'll be missed," she said. "And the hotel has terrible parking, anyway."

"Did you get a name, Fiona? A room number?"

"Michael, I can handle this myself," she said.

"That's my concern." My actual concern was that Fiona hadn't been set up innocently—or as innocently as anyone is set up to be shot by government agents—since it's not as if Fiona has kept a low profile since she arrived in Miami. If the ATF was interested in grabbing her, they could have gone to her condo, or they could have parked a detail of agents inside of my loft. None of it felt right. "Before you bang and burn the Hotel Oro," I said, "let's talk to Sam, see if he can find out anything."

Fiona sighed. "No spontaneity," she said. "You should try it, Michael. It wins girls' hearts."

Once you're out of the trade, there's not much you can do to earn a living that is remotely like what you've done before, unless you've been working under a cover during your years of service that actually entails a real job—liking hosting *The Gong Show*, for instance—and thus can just keep on working after you've been sunsetted out of your security clearances.

But if you've been flying around the world killing people and blowing up enemy targets, it's tough to slide behind a desk. Most spies are spies because they lack certain people skills:

Honesty.

Ethics.

Respect for property.

So your choices are generally limited. You can work for a paramilitary security group like Blackwater, which presents its own set of problems, not the least of which is that you can now get arrested for what you used to do legally. Like: Shooting people. You can get a job as a bodyguard for someone wealthy enough to require one. But wealthy people typically pay for crap, the reason they have so much money being that they don't squander it on things like expensive security details. Or you do what Sam Axe has done, which is live well by being the kind of man women want to sleep with, take care of and, occasionally, give a Cadillac to.

One of the first times I can recall working with Sam Axe was in the midnineties. We were in the Northern Caucasus Mountains training for an operation in Dagestan that ended up being aborted at the last moment. At the time, Sam still looked like the Navy SEAL he'd been—lean muscle mass stacked on a body fit for a linebacker—though he was under the employ of the Special Forces by then, mostly doing ops in the former USSR and the Middle East.

Figuring we had nothing to lose since the job was off anyway, we went to a bar Sam knew of in the village of Burl, about two dozen clicks from our base camp. Sam always knows of a bar. "Way I see it," Sam said then, "worst thing that could happen is we'd get into a fight and they'd know a team of Special Forces was hiding in the mountains preparing for some kind of armed action, and we'd end up on trial at the Hague.''

It seemed like a reasonable risk. By the end of the night, we were eating goat stew in a sprawling ranch house owned by a widow named Theckla, when Sam was seriously considering marrying. She promised him all the goat he could eat. For life. It didn't end well, of course.

He essentially washed out a few years ago, and now, if you were sitting across from Sam Axe, you might think he was a retired surfer: He favors Hawaiian shirts to camouflage, his muscles are covered by a subtle sheen of beer fat and he's let his hair grow out over his ears, where it's now touched with wisps of gray. All of his hard edges have been smoothed over with suntan oil, boat drinks and ocean views. He's technically still on the books with the government, but is mostly just playing out the string, taking the odd investigative job, which has dovetailed into us working together solving other people's problems.

Otherwise, his main job is to drink and sit in the sun . . . when he's not engaged watching me for the FBI. *Watching* is maybe a bit of a misnomer: It's more like proctoring, since there's nothing covert about what he's doing (at least not anymore—for the first few weeks, he made a go at being secretive, but then just told me he had to do it or they'd hold up his Navy pension), and his goal isn't so much to forbid me from doing anything as it is to make sure I don't piss off the FBI enough that they have me erased completely. He only gives the FBI what they want, but never volunteers information, which is fine. Having a friend as the conduit to the people who may eventually pull your card isn't so bad—it's not like he's the Stasi.

Plus, everyone needs to eat, and drink, maybe especially drink, which is what Sam was doing when I found him at the News Café. I called Sam just after meeting with Fiona to see if he could plug into a few of his sources to find out what the chatter was about the Oro. The thing about anyone with a security clearance is that they're like sixteen-year-old girls when you get down to their core. They all want to talk about the pretty outfit they did or didn't get, assign blame and start pulling hair.

Sam, well, he's got powers of persuasion. He can usually just pick up the phone and ask a question of these people—be they CIA, FBI, NSA or the most clandestine of all agencies, the DMV—and they'll at least tell him whom they're pissed at.

It was three o'clock and Sam sat facing the ocean, his shirt unbuttoned just enough so that passing tourists could see a few tufts of hair climbing up toward his Adam's apple. For a buck, he'd pose and let the savages take digital pictures. He was joined by five empty bottles of Corona, a ramekin filled with spent limes and a plate of congealed fat that might have once been cow based. I sat down across from him and tried to work the angle of the sun so that I wouldn't pick up the glare off of Sam's slimed over plate. I switched seats three times before giving up and putting on my sunglasses.

"You just missed Veronica," Sam said. Veronica was Sam's girlfriend, in the same way any woman has been Sam's girlfriend, which is to say she didn't have a strong opposition to congealed fats and beer, or at least Sam's particular charms outweighed the opposition. What those charms are, I've never been certain, except that I think he must excrete some kind of chemical in his sweat that attracts women with money. The same chemical also tends to attract women with husbands, which has caused problems in the past, though nothing Sam couldn't manage by kicking through a wall or two and running nude through the Everglades. That's one way of applying your specialized training in everyday life.

"A shame," I said. "We always have so much to talk about." The longest conversation I've ever had with Veronica consisted of her saying hello to me and me raising my eyebrows at her. It used to be that the fewer people I got to know personally, the less I might be disappointed by them later, but now it's just about convenience. "I hope she wasn't driving." I picked up one of the bottles of Corona and blew into it, making that humming sound. One of the perks of not constantly being in hiding anymore is that sometimes, just for the hell of it, I can act like a human.

"Oh, those are all mine," Sam said.

"You don't say. How many is that today?"

"Depends when you think *today* technically begins."

"Sunrise seems like a good starting point." Sam closed his eyes and started counting on his fingers; when he started doing laps around his thumb, I figured stopping him would make the day go easier on both of us. "Round off."

"About half," he concluded, which seemed right, since the day still had nine hours left in it. The difference between Sam Axe and most men is that alcohol doesn't seem to faze him much. No one ever claimed Sam wasn't complex. "Veronica's got a job for us," Sam said. "Friend of hers is in a bit of a jam."

"In a jam? What does that constitute, exactly?"

"You know," Sam said, "someone's in over their head. In a fix. In a bind. Needs a tall, dark stranger to make things right. All that."

"Let me guess," I said. "International terrorists? Peruvian gun cartels? Jehovah's Witnesses?"

"No." Sam squirmed in his chair. I'd come to talk to him about the incident at the Hotel Oro, and now here I was being put on the spot to help a friend of Veronica's, again, which wouldn't be so bad if they weren't the kind of people whose problems tended to start out as one thing and ended up as something else altogether. Rich people say it's all a mix-up with paperwork, and then, a couple days later, someone is trying to slit my throat.

"Well, that's a nice change. I'll guess again."

"Mikey . . ."

"Now, hold on, let me think. Drug dealers?"

"No," Sam said. "Forget it."

"No?"

"Not really."

"So, they're *sort of* drug dealers?"

"If you're not interested," Sam said, "I can handle the job myself."

"The last time you handled the job yourself," I said, "what was the final body count? Ten? Fifteen?"

"Which I thanked you for," Sam said.

"I don't like to kill people, Sam," I said. "I've got enough problems."

"They were all very bad," he said.

They were all bad—that was true—but a human life is a human life, and my sense is that I'm not living in a cartoon. Even the worst psychopath is someone's child, brother or sister, husband or wife or parent. If you have to kill someone to save your life, you kill them. But if you kill someone because it's easier than negotiating, you're no better than a dog that bites you just because it doesn't like your smell. It might be in your nature, but it doesn't make it the right thing to do. "Still," I said, "if I'm going to do whatever this is, I'd like to know that no one is going to be firing Scud missiles at my car."

"When did that ever happen?"

"Chechnya," I said. "After you broke up with the goat stew woman."

Sam made a noise that was somewhere in between a grunt and a sigh, which is about as close as Sam gets to true emotional response. "It's an easy job," Sam said, "I promise."

"You have no idea what the job is, do you?"

"I have a general outline," Sam said. "Like I said before: damsel in distress. That sort of thing. Besides, you owe me. I found out about your little party at the Hotel Oro."

"I was having lunch with my mother," I said. "It was Fiona's party."

"Kinky," Sam said, and then he broke down the particulars: An anonymous tip indicated that a courier would be arriving with a cache of assault rifles and ammunition—which was true—to be sold to certain Saudi nationals staying at the hotel. "The thing is, Mikey," he said, taking a swig from each of his five empty bottles, gathering up just enough backwash for a decent mouthful, "the caller had names. Big no-fly names. Fifteen different guys named Mohammed and Abdullah. They were already cleaning out cells at Gitmo. Dick Cheney was going to fly down and interrogate them himself, do a little water boarding. . . ."

I put a hand up. "I get it," I said. "Crazed fundamentalists." I grabbed up the five bottles and put them on the ground, lest my nausea from watching him drinking his own spit get the best of me. "Continue."

"Right," he said. He stared at the bottles a little mournfully until I literally snapped my fingers in front of his face to break the trance. "Well, anyway, they had the hotel scoped for those guys, but had no idea who Fiona was, only that they were looking for a woman carrying a bunch of heat."

"What about the crazed fundamentalists?"

"The block of rooms they'd booked was occupied by a sect of Elderhostel."

"Elderhostel?" I said. I flipped the name through my mind and nothing came flashing up. I hadn't been out of proper intelligence so long that an entire sect would have risen up without my knowledge, had I?

"Very dangerous group." Sam pulled out his wallet and rummaged through it for a moment, finally coming up with a glossy piece of paper he'd folded too many times. "This is how they recruit," he said, handing it to me. "Sophisticated bastards."

I unfolded the paper and learned that once I turn fifty-five, I'll be eligible to travel the world with 160,000 other active seniors in a continuing quest to educate themselves about the world via extraordinary learning adventures. "Who has access to the hotel's computer system?" I said.

"You'd have to get a subpoena for that information." Sam paused, which I took to mean he was going to let me process how clever it was that he knew I'd ask that, then that he expected me to ask him to do me a favor and try to find the information out in whatever way he could, since I clearly thought this was now something larger than Fiona, that it probably involved me and that someone was just using Fiona as a message to me, and then that he'd stun me with a reply on the subject that was abject in its thoroughness and that I would then thank him profusely for thinking of all the possible intangibles before I could even formulate a question.

So, instead, I just stared at him and waited. For a few minutes we actually sat there silently, until Sam finally got the hint that I wasn't going to bite and just opted to give me what I wanted to hear.

"They've got an eight hundred number that routes to a call center in Nebraska," he said. "They've got twenty-five in-house reservation clerks, another twenty-five front desk employees, then there're about fifty bellboys, half of whom have a record of some kind—petty stuff, mostly, though there's a guy parking cars who's actually got a pretty nice book running right now, even takes bets on Japanese Premier League soccer, who did a year for running a book I frequented a few years ago, which seems excessive, but that's just me, though it looks like he lied on his employment application and said he spent the last year studying abroad—and then there're the bartenders, cocktail and restaurant staff, too, and then the whole executive branch and probably a few corporate people who, with just a few keystrokes, could find out anything they wanted about anyone staying at the hotel."

"Good customer service," I said. If you ever want to start stealing identities for a living but have an aversion to sifting through trash or aren't especially good at hacking into personal computers, get a job at a hotel. People on vacation are stupid. They trust everyone with a name tag. Walk up to a person sitting poolside and ask them to confirm their room number by giving you the last four digits of their social security number and most likely they'll give you all nine, because everyone recites the entire number in order to get to those four numbers. Barring that, come by the next time and ask for the first five numbers. Ask them for a special PIN number for the hotel voice mail, and you'll likely get their ATM PIN, too. Ask them to surrender their passport, give a vial of blood and a cup of urine and, if you asked nicely and promised them a robe and a mint, you're unlikely to get any sort of resistance whatsoever.

And if you don't want to get an actual job, just get a name tag.

"Three hundred," Sam said.

"Three hundred?"

"That's how many people—give or take—have access to the system," Sam said.

Three hundred people, but only one had a reason to set up Fiona, but not enough reason to actually give out her name or her description. Three hundred people who might have had access to anyone dumb enough to give up their information and change it to the names of known terrorists, but only one who'd actually know those names. Three hundred people and only one who might reasonably want to send me a message by using Fiona without getting her killed in the process, making it all so obvious that only someone completely untrained and unknown would walk into it.

"Who owns the hotel?" I asked.

"Shareholders," he said, but he said it in the same way he told me I'd need to get a subpoena.

"Are we going to do this again," I said, "or are you just going to jump right to the part where I realize who is currently in Miami that might want to kill me?"

"It's owned primarily by an Eastern European conglomerate," Sam said.

"That's not terribly specific," I said. "If I have to boil down who might want to send me a message to half of a continent, I'll be dead before you're able to flag down the waitress again."

"I saw a lot of Russian names," Sam said. "Wouldn't it be nice if they could just forgive and forget? We won, you lost, not too many people died in the process, sit down, have a drink of vodka, put on a pair of Levi's, call it a game."

"Tell that to Putin," I said.

"Putin," Sam said. He spit the Russian president's name out like it hurt. "I ever tell you what a crap shot he was?"

"No less than a hundred times," I said. The fact was the former Soviet Union was one of my main theaters of operation. The other fact is that apart from Cubans, the majority of organized crime in and around Miami belongs to the Russians. A few years ago they made a strategic alliance with the Colombian drug cartels, the result being that the Colombians supply the product, the Russians supply the money and the muscle. Along the way, just like the good little capitalists they've become, they've bought into real estate, gobbling up shopping centers, hotels, nightclubs, entire neighborhoods. You move your money around enough, build legit businesses to shelter and protect it, invest in real estate, line the pockets of county commissioners, make donations to congressional campaigns, maybe drop a grand to the ACLU and the SPCA, too, and people tend to forget that it all started with cocaine, and heroin and all they see is the gentrification your money provides.

"I don't know the veracity of this," Sam said, "because you understand the boys were a little embarrassed that they kicked in a bunch of doors and pistol-whipped a few seniors, but no one in the hotel's management put up any stink. Repaired the doors, fixed things right back up and that was that. Even gave a few of the agents vouchers for free massages."

"This doesn't scan," I said. Fiona gets contacted for a gun buy and it turns out it's a sting, but no one gets stung? Hundred different people they could have gone through, big-timers, and they pick Fi? And just let her walk. And then the specific names of terrorists.

One of the first things you learn about being a spy is that there is no chaos. Everything that appears random and disorganized but ultimately disastrous is likely to have a deep and intricate network of connective lines holding it all together. People walking down the street see a man in a suit running, and they think he's late for a meeting. On the next block, they see a woman screaming into a cell phone, and they thing she's having a bad day. And when they get to their office and it's been cordoned off with crime tape, they think maybe someone killed themselves and took out a few coworkers in the process.

I see possibility, connection, locus points.

I stood up and dropped a twenty on the table, which would cover at least another round or two.

"Maybe it's not about you," Sam said.

"Maybe," I said.

"Maybe it's all a big coincidence," Sam said.

"Maybe," I said.

"Maybe you're going to go over there and find out anyway?"

"Definitely," I said. I looked down at the table and saw that the twenty was already gone. Sam's like a cat.

"You want me to go with you?"

"No," I said. "If it's nothing, it's nothing. If it's something, it's probably something you don't need to be a part of."

Sam nodded. I knew if I needed Sam, he'd be there, but at this point it seemed prudent to find out for myself what was waiting for me. If it had to do with my burn notice, bringing along Sam wouldn't help things.

"Listen, Mikey, this thing with Veronica's friend . . ."

"What time, Sam?"

"I told her we'd be at her place tomorrow morning at nine."

I checked my watch. It was just short of three

thirty. The sun was still full in the sky. "You going to stay up all night?"

Sam considered that idea for a moment, giving it more credence than I thought possible. "I guess maybe I'll try to turn in early," he said. "You want your twenty back?"

"Keep it," I said, walking out, "in case I need to make bail later."

2

There are four basic kinds of surveillance: static, foot, mobile and technical. If you're just a regular person, these are also the four basic ways you can stalk someone. The difference between the two classifications is semantic: No matter if you're a spy, or if you're insane and think reruns of *Magnum P.I.* are telling you to follow Tom Selleck, the goal of surveillance is to learn as much about your target as possible while not revealing your position until you have sufficient information on how to proceed.

Static surveillance requires planning and takes monastic patience. You want to find a place with concealed points of entry and exit, preferably one in a rectangular shape so you can place yourself against one wall and see everything around you without impediment. You want visual access to your target. Unless you like wearing adult diapers, you want a toilet nearby. Access to food is nice, since it's unlikely you'll be ordering up pizzas or cooking your favorite pot roast.

I've always been partial to static surveillance since it allows you to process repeated action, opening windows into how a particular person or group operates when they think no one is watching them. Under ideal conditions, that's how I would have approached identifying the mystery target inside the Hotel Oro.

But I figured they already knew I was coming, so why worry about finding the perfect-fitting adult diaper?

The entrance of the Hotel Oro is cut out of black-and-gold marble accented by a team of valets and bellboys wearing black Armani suits. I guess the outfits are supposed to engender confidence in those leaving cars and luggage in the care of these men, since if the valets and bellboys wear Armani, what must the rest of the place be like? Then there's the common presumption that well-dressed people aren't criminals, though of course if you're any good at crime, you can probably afford a decent pair of shoes and a nice pair of slacks. Outlet stores have really evened the playing field—even your garden-variety asshole can get an off-season Armani suit, or, in the case of paroled felons, hotels in Miami are kind enough to provide them gratis.

I've always preferred to get mine in Italy.

As soon as I pulled my black 'seventy-four Dodge Charger up to the valet station in front of the hotel, a valet descended on me.

"Staying the night, sir?" the valet asked. He looked
at the Charger like it was covered in smallpox, as if
he was so used to parking Bentleys that he couldn't
conceive of a reason anyone would deign to roll in
a car made in America and at least a decade before
he was born. He tugged on my door but I hadn't
unlocked it. This seemed to confound him even
more.

"No," I said.

"If you're making a delivery," he said, his voice
losing any of the politeness his *very nice* Armani suit
would indicate was bred into him, "receiving is
around back."

I smiled, because sometimes it's fun to smile at
those who condescend to you because they think
their job assigns them some social importance. I took
a brief inventory of the valet: diamond studs in his
ears, an absurd jade pinky ring, one of those crusted
gold watches that pimps and gamblers prefer. I had
a pretty good idea that this was one of the men on
Sam's list of former and current felons. The neck tat-
toos were also a good indication. "Let me ask you
something," I said. "You ever do any time?"

The valet cocked his head like a golden retriever
and then leaned into my window. He had this sneer
on his face that I thought made him look like he was
suffering from a kidney stone, like maybe he'd been
pissing blood and vomiting all day, or had maybe
accidentally swallowed lighter fluid, but which probably scared a lot of people not used to seeing how
people really looked when they were angry. The one

thing about being a spy and knowing how to really hurt people, which this guy probably thought he knew how to do, too, was that it's always nice feeling vaguely feared and respected at the same time, even if it's unearned. "Who the fuck are you?"

I got out of the car without any covert movement whatsoever, knocking the valet back a few steps. I handed him my keys and a ten dollar bill. "The guy whose car you're parking," I said. There was a row of luxury cars lined up in a perfect diagonal to the entrance a few yards away, as if passing tourists would see the Mercedes phalanx and simply drop dead from envy. "Keep it close to the front, maybe move one of those Mercedes, give me the over on the Dolphins and, when you get the chance, maybe visit HR and correct some of the errors on your résumé."

I turned my back on the valet and walked toward the entrance, though I could still feel his eyes on me, likely trying to figure out if I was a cop, a rival or just a particularly enlightened member of the hotel's management. Or maybe he just liked the cut of my suit.

The inside of the Oro looks like a perfume commercial. You walk in and to your left is a sunken bar filled with bone white couches set in relief by bronzed women wearing mostly their own flesh and men who seem to be waiting for the photo shoot to begin. Morning, noon or night, these people are sitting on the couches, idly drinking martinis or eating finger foods that are more accurately fingernail foods. To the right is another bar, this one decorated like a bedroom you could never sleep in: twenty cabanas shrouded in white silk house plush king-sized beds covered in a *Caligula* of bodies and white chenille pillows, a fluffy sofa and a small bedside table. These then encircle a dance floor that always seems to be playing a song about hustling coke, whores, strippers or coke whore strippers.

In order to get to the registration desk, you have to walk through the middle of these two bars, which might be why so few people ever end up checking in. It's not a family environment, unless you're practicing to make one, which is why I should have been curious from the get-go that my mother wanted to dine there this afternoon, but sometimes, with my mother, it's better to just nod your head and agree than to actually listen and interpret.

The registration desk isn't actually a desk. It's a twelve-foot-long S-shaped aquarium filled with goldfish, though no actual goldfish, and the people standing behind it all look fashionably bored tapping away at computers or talking on their Bluetooths. I walked up to the one fashionably bored person who wasn't otherwise engaged. She was about twenty-five, looked about sixteen, and probably thought I looked a hundred.

"I'm Michael Westen," I said.

The girl nodded once, tapped a few keys on her keyboard and handed me a room key without looking back up. "Ms. Copeland is expecting you in room one fifty-three," she said. "She also asks that if you have a gun, to leave it in our safe."

I smiled, because, sometimes, when you're faced with the absurd, it's good to do just that sort of thing. "That's not going to happen," I said. I slid the room key back across the aquarium. "What's option two?"

The girl started tapping on the keyboard again, still not looking up, which was too bad because I was still smiling. "Yes, Mr. Westen, I see," she said. "Ms. Copeland is expecting you in cabana six."

I turned around in time to see two security guards yank three writhing bodies from a cabana. "Will the sheets be changed?" I asked.

"Of course, Mr. Westen," she said. She tapped something on her keyboard again.

"What are you typing?"

The girl stopped typing, but still didn't look up. "Nothing, Mr. Westen," she said.

"Then why are you typing?"

"Just following Ms. Copeland's directions," she said.

I leaned over the aquarium and turned the computer monitor so I could see it. Under *Special Instructions* it said: *Keep typing until Mr. Westen leaves the counter. Do not make eye contact.* I spun the monitor back so that it faced the girl.

"What's your name?" I said.

"Star," she said. She was already typing again.

You never meet a woman in Miami named Sue anymore. An entire generation of women has decided that adopting stripper names sounds somehow more interesting. "What's your real name?" I said.

The typing paused. "Joanne," she said quietly.

"Joanne," I said, "look at me."

The girl tilted her eyes up but her head remained firmly downcast. "I'm just trying to do my job," she said.

"I understand that," I said, "but your job sucks. Now lift your head up and look at my face." Joanne did as I asked. "My name is Michael Westen. I have a gun—that's true—but in my case it's okay. I have a license. Or, well, I did. It's confusing. My point is this, Joanne: you need to quit your job the next time you're asked to tell someone to stow their gun in the company safe. You understand that that request is not normal, don't you, Joanne? You understand that if you ask the wrong person to do that, it's likely they'll shoot you in the face, don't you, Joanne?"

"I guess," she said.

"There's no guessing here. You either understand or you don't."

"Okay, yeah, I understand."

"Good," I said. "Now, Joanne, tell me something. Have you ever met Ms. Copeland?"

"Of course," she said. "She's the general manager. I see her every Tuesday, Thursday and Saturday. I'm trying to get on Wednesdays, too, but things have been so hectic with my modeling and stuff, but it's, like, a toss-up, you know, because I can go on an audition or I can just be here and hope that someone notices me. . . ."

In addition to having the names of strippers, every woman in Miami is trying to be a model, which I've always thought was like aspiring to be a mannequin. Who would be interested in someone who posed their entire life? If there's one thing that has always returned me to Fiona, eventually, it's that the only photos of her in print have been where she's in the background of some burning wreckage. "Joanne," I said, "stop speaking." She did. "How long have you worked here?"

"Forever."

"How long is forever these days?"

"Almost a month."

"And has Ms. Copeland been here the whole time?"

Joanne, who, really, should have rechristened herself Black Hole if she wanted to be more personally accurate, tapped a finger against her chin. I waited while she thought things through, though I had a pretty good sense already of what I was walking into. The Hotel Oro had all the hallmarks of the perfect cover job for an operative—a transient population of employees, most of whom were just waiting for that big break (which likely meant that they were hoping *The Real World* put out a casting call), guests who didn't stay long enough to notice anything peculiar and a job that generally required no work whatsoever.

"I think she got here two weeks ago," Joanne finally decided, though it sounded absolutely possible that Joanne could be wrong, possible that Ms. Copeland's first day started about five hours previous.

"Thank you, Joanne," I said. "Why don't you

check your computer and see if Ms. Copeland has given you the okay to let me walk over to the cabana?''

Joanne clicked away. "Yes, Mr. Westen, your cabana is ready."

"Excellent," I said. "You may now resume staring idly at your keypad and typing, if you don't think it's too late to keep your job."

Joanne shrugged. "Whatever," she said. "I've got an audition for an Abercrombie shoot after work today, anyway."

I would have wished Joanne good luck, but my sense was that if I were to wish her anything, it would have less to do with luck and more to do with common sense, but I've found wishing people good common sense is rarely a nice way to depart. So, instead, I just gave her a little nod meant to connote a larger, deeper understanding between the two of us.

Besides, my larger concern at that point was trying to figure out who this Ms. Copeland really was. The name "Copeland" made me think she was British, but British agents rarely have anything against their American counterparts, apart from armory envy. When you're working undercover, it's important to keep your backstory as close to your own as possible so that you don't trip yourself up being more convoluted than you need to be. If you like pepper steak in real life, so does your cover. If you went to high school in Miami in the 1980s, so did your cover. And if your last name is Copeland in cover, then your real last name probably is something very close to that as well, at least something that sounds like it, even better if your cursive scrawl might normally approximate the same letters, too. You spend your entire life signing your name one way and then suddenly have to sign an entirely different name, and it's likely you'll screw up at least once, and one time is all it will take to get you killed. In addition, even a halfway decent handwriting specialist would be able to point out the pregnant pauses in your penmanship, the deliberation over a letter that you'd normally move fluidly through, and could thus point you out as a fraud.

I ran the name through my head, chopped off letters, thought about different iterations and decided that, in about thirty seconds, I was going to either have a chat with an old friend or I was going to be strangled to death with a bedsheet. If the person was who I thought it was going to be, there wouldn't be much wiggle room between the two, but I did think it was unlikely that any employee of the hotel—be it just a cover or not—would want to try to explain the bloodstains all over so much fine white fabric.

Standing in front of my assigned cabana was one of those guys who think lifting weights will make him a good fighter. Lifting weights will make you strong. Lifting weights will make you lose fat and gain muscle. Lifting weights will not give you a strong chin or teach you how to defend yourself when someone who weighs a hundred pounds less than you is punching you in the throat. To be a good fighter, flexibility is an asset, whereas muscle mass will help you if someone tries to stab you, but won't change anything if they poke you in the eye. Guys like this, your average bouncer, might know how to get someone drunk and stupid to submit, or they might have the strength to pick you up and throw you through a window, but they're probably no use to anyone if you happen to kick them in the knee. Bulky muscle is slow. Lean, manicured muscle is fast. You want lean and manicured.

Naturally though, he, too, wore an Armani suit, except his bulged along the seams of his shoulders and knees, and he'd accented the outfit with a black Under Armour T-shirt so that I could actually make out each hair on his chest. I didn't notice any weapon on him, apart from what I learned was stunning intellect.

"You Michael Westen?" he said when I approached. Actually, it was more like a low grumble. They must have an employee training program at the Oro that requires their security guards to speak with gravel in their mouth for a week before taking the floor.

"Why do people forget verbs when they're trying to sound intimidating?" I asked.

"Yes or no?" he said. I tried to get a peek around him, but he was so wide that I couldn't quite see inside the cabana. All I could make out was a single leg, which was all I really needed to see anyway.

"There you go again," I said.

"Just let him in," came an exasperated voice from inside the cabana. It had a British accent, which was new, but not unexpected. The guard gave me a little glare—not enough to actually cause me any offense, but enough to inform me that he didn't know what a verb was and therefore thought I'd really insulted him—and then swept open the rest of the thin curtain to reveal Ms. Copeland sitting aside the bed on the small sofa.

Except that it wasn't Ms. Copeland.

Oh, it was Ms. Copeland as Joanne knew her and as the meat standing in front of the cabana knew her, but to me she was Natalya Choplyn. The last time I saw her was in Bulgaria.

She tried to poison me.

"What a surprise," I said.

"Is it really?" Natalya said.

"No," I said. I was still standing in the entrance to the cabana, trying to figure out where I was going to sit. It was either unfold myself on the bed, which seemed not only compromising but presumptuous, or sit directly next to Natalya on the couch, which was really more of a love seat, which, really, is just a fancy name for a big chair not made for two spies who've slept with each other *and* tried to seriously hurt each other. I decided just to stand.

"I don't bite," she said, patting the space next to her.

"You do stab," I said. Natalya shrugged. Not much you can do with the truth but accept it. "I like the accent. Let me guess: Sandringham, Norfolk?"

"Conveys a sense of elegance, don't you think?"

"It's so simple," I said. "Where's the challenge?"

"Worked for Princess Di, didn't it?"

"I suppose," I said, "though I've always thought of you more like Camilla. Maybe move across the country, say you're from Wales. Thicken your vowels a bit and aim for more of that singsong style and you'll have it nailed."

"Do I not sound convincing?"

"It will work here," I said. "But I doubt it will fly in an interrogation. A couple of well-placed electrodes and you'll be screaming *Nyet! Nyet!* in no time."

"Is that what you'd do to me, Michael? Electrodes? I don't believe that's covered by your Geneva Conventions." Natalya stood then and walked a few steps to the marble nightstand beside the bed, where there was a silver teakettle and two cups. She was taller than I remembered, though the last time I saw her we were stooped over in a cave, which always makes everyone seem slightly more diminutive than usual. Her hair then was short and black and likely still was, since her hair on this day was shoulder-length and deep red, which made me presume it was a wig. An expensive wig, but a wig no less. She wore a perfectly tailored black Gucci suit, alligator and lambskin Chanel pumps and had tasteful diamonds on each ear, around her neck and, notably, on her wedding-ring finger.

"I'm not exactly covered by the Geneva Conventions, either," I said. Natalya's back was still to me as she poured the tea, but I thought I saw something slacken in her posture. There was no use lying to

Natalya, since she thought, for some reason, that she needed to see me, which likely meant that she thought I'd crossed her in some way and was giving me the professional courtesy of asking me about it before she blew up my car with me in it. Telling her I was out of work would likely cause her to reevaluate whatever her specific beef was.

"I heard you were still under contract," she said.

"I got burned," I said. Natalya dunked a cube of sugar into each cup of tea, turned back around and offered me one of the cups. "The last time I saw you, you poisoned me."

"You didn't die."

"I spent three days in a hospital," I said.

"Suit yourself." Natalya stepped past me, her shoulder brushing my chest, instructed her security guard to pin both sides of the curtain up so we could have a view of the dance floor and then handed the guard the second cup of tea and told him his services were no longer needed. As he walked off, he sipped absently at the tea and didn't once convulse. "Now," she said, settling back down on the sofa, "where were we?"

"You were just about to explain to me why you used Fiona and two dozen armed agents to let me know you were in town," I said.

"I never understood what you saw in that terrorist," she said.

"She's not a terrorist," I said. "Not even an enemy combatant. Not technically."

"Oh, that's right," Natalya said. "The IRA is a

peaceful, nonviolent organization. Like Amnesty International, only with car bombs."

"Just like the KGB was," I said. "And we're no longer dating, so there's that."

A smirk danced around the edges of Natalya's mouth. "Really?"

"Really."

"And yet here you are," she said.

"That's a nice ring you have," I said. "Did you and the president of Albania finally make it official?"

Natalya lifted her hand and made a show of the diamond. "A prop," she said. "Just like your precious Fiona."

"What are we doing here, Natalya?"

"Catching up," she said. "Reviving an old friendship."

"You could have sent me an e-mail," I said. "You didn't need to set up Fiona."

"Yes," Natalya said, "I'm sorry about that. But she's a smart girl, that Fiona. I knew she wouldn't get caught. I didn't realize you and your lovely mother would be there, too. She seemed to be having a splendid time. Shame she didn't get to enjoy her lunch. I oversaw the preparation of her salad myself. And I think you would have enjoyed your egg whites."

You always want to put your opponent on edge, thinking their very next step might be their last. People don't want to die. People who want to die are mentally ill, sociopaths or think a heaven of milk, honey and countless ready-for-hot-sex virgins awaits them. People, normal people, will opt to live. People, normal people, who try to kill themselves, will often receive an involuntary physical override via the human reset button known as blacking out. Above all else, people don't want to die. So they give up information. They say things to save themselves. They put faith in the humanity of others in hopes of being spared. The trained eye will see the truth. The trained eye will watch for tells, for shimmers that seep out involuntarily, things said to make a person worry.

Bringing in family is generally considered poor form, particularly if you're doing sanctioned work, since killing civilians is frowned upon.

That Natalya brought up my mother was a tell.

That Natalya brought up my mother was also a bluff.

First problem: Natalya Choplyn isn't a normal person. Dying to her would probably be considered upsetting but expected. After spending two decades working first for the KGB and then later the FSB and then, well, whatever agency Putin had her fronting in, occupational hazards are fairly terminal.

Second problem: If Natalya Choplyn really wanted me dead, as seems to be the case more and more frequently with people I encounter—a disturbing trend, certainly—she could have done so that morning as I sat with my mother, my guard whittled down by the persistent gnaw of my mother's voice.

Third problem: All of this had transpired in public.

Natalya needed something. Maybe she wanted something, too, but above all else, there was need.

"I'm leaving," I said. "See you at your war crimes trial."

"Please wait," Natalya said. She reached out and grabbed my arm. Not hard. Not insistent. Softly.

Need it was.

I looked at my watch. "Five minutes," I said.

Natalya nodded slightly. "Will you sit?"

History told me that I shouldn't trust Natalya. We were both sent to Bulgaria to take care of the same problem: Vitaly Sigal. Sigal was a low-level administrator at the Kremlin when the Russians entered Afghanistan in 1978, but since he spoke Farsl he ended up getting a cushy assignment in the country, which he turned into an even cushier black market career that extended to buying and selling large arms and propellants throughout the Middle East during the nineties. When the building blocks of the Iraqi Tammuz-1 missile were traced to a few key purchases made through Sigal, I was dispatched to find him.

When I finally found Sigal, he was holed up in the Dryanovo Monastery as a guest of the monks. Natalya had likewise been sent as protection, since word of his worth on the world market had made its way to the people who had lingering interests in Sigal not landing in U.S. hands, not that that was what my orders were, precisely. I'd encountered Natalya on several other occasions—Chechnya, Bucharest, twice in France, once outside a nuclear sub docked in San Francisco, once Christmas shopping in Dubai—and though we'd never tried to kill each other directly, there was a sense of general animosity that broiled between us by virtue of nationalistic genetics and a few "incidents" involving guns, Black Hawks and covert operations involving oil, of course. One on one, on even ground (Dubai), we'd had a few drinks which turned into a few more drinks, which turned into, well, *something*. Sometimes, it's safer having sex with someone you know absolutely is the enemy.

But in Bulgaria, there would be none of that. I wanted Sigal or at least certain information he could provide. She wanted to protect Sigal. We agreed to meet in the Bacho Kiro caves, an ancient labyrinth of caves located above the monastery where Sigal was housed. For the first two days, we negotiated off and on for hours in the stone forest section of the cave, the tourists milling past us none the wiser that two superpowers were trading information, making concessions, looking at the soft points of each other's musculature. On the third day, Natalya produced Sigal and allowed me to interrogate him for several hours . . . and then, well, she tried to poison me.

I stepped out of the cabana, found a bar stool and dragged it back in front of the opening. "Talk," I said.

"It seems we have a problem," she said. "I've been informed that I'm marked for expulsion from this life, never mind my present position."

"Not my problem," I said.

"But it is," she said. Natalya explained that her sources had informed her that I'd implicated her in concert with the Colombians; that she'd been the point person in a long-running drug enterprise, through the Port of Miami and Panama, all under the Russian flag without sharing in the profits. A big no-no, even to the Russians.

And, moreover, that I'd been the facilitator, had my own hands in this business, and had flipped information on Natalya to save my own life.

"That's not true," I said. "And if you thought it was true, we wouldn't be sitting here. And if you were doing it, you wouldn't care if I'd implicated you or not. You can disappear just as easily as you've appeared here."

"Things have changed, Michael," she said.

It was hard to tell when Natalya was lying, but something in her voice seemed tickled, as if there was a real person beneath the old Cold War exterior. I looked around the floor of the bar, at the beautiful people milling about, at the bumping and the grinding, at the common luxury, the thugs and dealers looking unimpressed across the way, the Armani suits, the diamonds, the gold, the drinks, the absolute benign-ness of it all, compared to the life Natalya had already lived. Her cover had always involved the travel industry—in Dubai, she ran a resort for the sultan—but this wasn't travel. It was excess. And it wasn't even remotely interesting.

But there was something more. I looked again at Natalya, tried to really see her. She'd been a flawless beauty before—if that's possible—with an intellect equal to anyone I'd come up against. She was also relentless, always in motion.

Sitting on a love seat in a cabana would be like being submerged underwater.

Her body back in the day was all coiled muscle, but I thought I saw the tiniest roll around her midsection.

I snapped my hand out and grabbed her left wrist. She didn't flinch.

I put my thumb and forefinger around her wedding ring, all two carats of it, and pulled, but there was little budge. I let go of her hand and sat back on the bar stool. Natalya hadn't moved an inch. "Boy or girl?" I asked.

"One of both," she said.

"That's good," I said. "Me and my brother, it was always a competition, never a friendship. Even today, there's that space between us. Brothers and sisters, it's more protective."

"I hope they don't need to be protected."

"You made the wrong career choices," I said. "There will always be someone out there, Natalya."

She nodded once.

"The way I look at it," I said, "you have something to lose, you maybe make a concerted effort to avoid conflicts that might bubble out into your real life. You come after someone's family, that changes things. You maybe try to get out of the life you've made. You don't threaten people who could make your children motherless."

Natalya exhaled and I realized that the entire time we'd been talking, she'd been taking only the tiniest of breaths. You can train yourself to do anything, but it's difficult to override the nervous system. "Be that as it may," she said, "the information I have comes from a very good source. Until I see proof otherwise, I have to trust my source."

"Let me guess. A mole in the FBI? A mole in the CIA? A mole in the NSA? It's a lie, Natalya. I've got so many problems right now, the last thing I need is to be selling out other agents, even ones who tried to poison me."

"I've been given the courtesy of a week's time to settle this situation," she said.

"Let me guess. You either come up with the missing money or proof that it's a lie or you're dead. Would that be accurate?"

"Somewhat," she said.

"Oh, wait," I said. "There are pictures somewhere, would that be correct? Or, better, someone is taking pictures right this very moment." Natalya indicated that was the case. "So now I'm not only burned— I'm also potentially a double agent?"

"That wasn't too difficult for you," Natalya said.

"This has been a great year," I said. "There any job openings here at the hotel? Maybe something working security, where I could just mumble and threaten people?"

"A friendly contact operates the hotel chain," she said. "You always liked Albania, didn't you, Michael?"

"What do you need from me, Natalya?"

Natalya took a sip of her tea. "Proof. Barring that, the missing cut."

"That's not going to happen," I said.

"I have my orders then." She set her tea down and got up, smoothed lint from her skirt and smiled at me in a way I found rather disconcerting. Nothing seemed all that happy. "It was lovely to see you, Michael. The years have certainly been your friend. It's a shame, really, to stay looking so good when the world has grown so ugly. It makes you stand out." She patted me on the knee as she walked past and for a moment I thought that Fiona was probably right from the get-go: Blowing up the hotel would have been easier.

3

The next day, Sam picked me up at eight thirty in the morning. He was clean shaven, his pants looked pressed and his shirt was absent any sort of floral or fruit arrangements. I looked into the backseat and noticed an actual blazer, still in the dry cleaner's bag. When I slid into his Cadillac, he handed me a plastic grocery bag.

"What's this?" I asked.

"I took the liberty of picking you up breakfast," he said, "just to show you how much I appreciate you taking time out of your busy schedule to assist me in this venture."

In the bag were two dozen containers of yogurt. Some were even flavors I liked.

"Coming on a little thick this morning," I said.

"You think?"

"Is there already a complication in your damsel-in-distress scenario?"

"I went by last night and met the damsel," he said.

"Cricket O'Connor is her name. She's . . . challenging."

"Excellent," I said. "That's exactly what I'm looking for. More challenging women with problems." I told Sam about my meeting the previous day at the Hotel Oro, about the rather precarious situation it revealed and how it presented a few fresh issues for me to deal with, not the least of which was trying to figure out who would provide false information to the Russians in my name, and why. Sam would have the contacts to get to some of the truth, but in times like these, a little financial grease would probably be needed.

And, as usual, apart from the thousands and thousands of dollars in my frozen bank accounts, I didn't have much money, a fact that seemed to make Sam happier than I would have liked.

"Then this job we have is coming at just the right time," Sam said.

The Miami I grew up in isn't the one I returned to. I knew this before, but on this day, as Sam drove us through the neighborhoods surrounding my place and then east on the Dolphin Expressway toward the MacArthur Causeway, where we'd pick up a private ferry to take us to Fisher Island, where Sam's said damsel (one Cricket O'Connor) lived, I couldn't help but notice how little I recognized this as home. A normal kid, maybe he sees all the tourist points of Miami before he turns twelve, goes to the Orange Bowl, maybe takes in the Art Deco tour, sees the

Blue Angels at the Air and Sea Show, watches the Winterfest Boat Parade.

By twelve, I was sure my father wasn't just a bully but a bastard, that my mother was her own particular kind of horror show and that my brother, Nate, would always complicate things.

By twelve, I'd already stolen a dozen cars.

By twelve, I was already figuring out how to get the hell out.

Miami has always been a city of rogues and ruffians—that much is certain—but in the twenty years since I left town for good, only to return for a day or two at a time, though not long enough to actually be there when my father finally died, leaving my mother to her paranoia and Nate to, well, Nate, it's become this odd mix of glitz and sham, so that even the humble neighborhood I grew up in is a mark for those who want to speed into town and speed back out with cash in their pockets.

Real estate, once a bargain, has turned into the irresistible boom, impervious to the real world, since the people with six million dollars to spend on a waterfront home aren't carrying subprime loans and surely don't live in the real world. Crockett and Tubbs couldn't stop the drugs and neither has anyone else, the cocaine trade becoming a cash crop far more lucrative than sugar and just as easily attained, so in came even more drugs, like heroin, and cheaper drugs, like meth, all of which then fed and grew until Miami became not just the party capital of the country but also the center for identity theft, murder and narcoterrorism.

Ah, home.

With all of those things comes another kind of evil, or at least one of the more egregious sins: envy. You can't be too rich in Miami; you always have to have something more than your neighbor, always have to live somewhere even more extravagant, so that your wealth isn't merely the end result of your hard work—it's the hole card that provides the flush of other people's envy.

"You know what I wonder?" Sam asked. We were on the private ferry—which is pejorative to ferries, since this was more like a cruise liner that happened to carry expensive cars, along with the few clunkers belonging to the help, or just the help themselves, most too poor to own cars—halfway between the causeway and Fisher Island at this point, but had opted to get out of Sam's car to take on the view of the private isle.

"I can't even pretend to know."

"You see all of these minimum-wage people? They spend all day on this little slab of paradise, and they'll never, at the rate they're going, ever have enough money to even own a blade of grass on the island."

"Yeah?"

"So why do they even bother? Why even wake up in the morning when you know that you're always going to be crawling out of the same rut, until you're too old for that rut, and then you'll be forced to get into an even worse rut?"

"Everyone needs a job," I said. "Look at us."

"Naw," he said, "what we did was make it so everyone could feel safe in their crappy lives, and for what, really? Float out here from Cuba for a better life and end up working for some rich despot just the same."

"That's capitalism at work," I said.

Sam stared out over the water and squinted, as if he were trying to see something that wasn't there. "Listen," he said, "this thing with Natalya Choplyn, that's not something to trifle with."

"I know, Sam."

"Mikey, she might have impressed you with her husband and family but she's still calling shots around the world," he said. "She saw your mother. If Fiona hadn't been on top of her game, she'd be dead and probably two or three dozen other people would be too. The kind of juice she must have to get the no-call names, to get actual agents out on this, that means whoever told her you dimed her is big. Let's just pull the plug here, let the CIA know she's here and go on with our lives. You don't have to let this concern you."

Sam was probably right. But I'd been threatened.

"You don't think the CIA knows where she is? They've probably been tracking her on Echelon for fifteen years," I said. "And you don't think she'd be a step ahead of us? Waiting for that? If her source is so good, it probably *is* CIA." But there was something more, something that niggled at my mind, an inkling that whoever was trying to get her out by using me was involved with my burn notice and that, if I solved this, I might have one more piece of the puzzle fixed. And then there was the likelihood that somewhere there were pictures of us palling around Dubai and I'd be tried as a traitor and hanged, all of which I mentioned to Sam, as well, and which didn't sound like a great way to spend an afternoon.

Sam digested all of that. "Then let me help you, at least."

"Are we having a little bit of a moment here?"

"Little bit, yeah."

I patted him on the back. "You're hired," I said. An announcement rang over the PA system that we'd be docking on Fisher Island in five minutes, that we should be mindful of the island's strict twenty-five-mile-per-hour speed limit and that the temperature on the island was a perfect eighty-two degrees. "Maybe, if things work out, we can get ourselves a blade of grass out here to retire on."

Prior to 1905, Fisher Island didn't exist. But when the dredging project to create a shipping lane into Miami left a couple hundred acres of green island adrift in Biscayne Bay, the island was born. What was once just mangroves became a millionaire's retreat, the property shifting hands between some of the nation's wealthiest people, eventually ending up in the hands of the Vanderbilts, before turning into what it is now: the most exclusive address in Miami.

As Sam drove towards Cricket O'Connor's house, we passed the private resort that was once the Vanderbilt estate and is now a playground for those for whom price is no problem, replete with towering coconut trees, a distinctly Gatsby-ish expanse of tennis courts and a rippling golf course peopled by men wearing sweaters tied over their shoulders, as if a squall were just around the corner. A ten-story condo complex hugged the coastline and offered astonishing views starting at two million dollars. Along the narrow avenues were elaborate guard gates and surprisingly tasteful manors, usually with a design mirroring the old Vanderbilt estate—Spanish influences abounded with a neo–Art Deco flair tossed in for flavor.

From the moment we drove off the ferry, I counted seven Bentleys, fifteen Mercedes, two dozen face-lifts, double that many boob jobs (usually on women more accustomed to being called Bubby than Baby) and enough tummy tucks and lip implants to make one wonder how anyone functions with the fat cells they were born with.

The air was warm.

The streets perfectly clean.

The views were impeccable.

It was, frankly, making me a little paranoid.

But then I had the strangest memory.

"I've actually been here before," I said.

"You're thinking of Grenada," Sam said. "The

night before the invasion, right? It was just like this. Helluva time. Female med students have special needs in times of war, if you know what I'm saying."

"I was in eighth grade when we invaded Grenada," I said.

"A shame," Sam said. "We could have used you. You know, I still have a tiny piece of shrapnel in my left big toe from that. Cold days, it's like someone's sticking a fork into my foot."

It was probably very near the time Sam was storming the beach that I was last on Fisher Island, though it didn't look quite like it did on this day, at least not in my memory. My father and mother were fighting, throwing dishes and frozen food at each other, so Nate and I sneaked out of the house and just rode the buses around Miami. Nate had stolen a bunch of transfer passes, so we ended up going clear across the city and found ourselves at the very marina Sam and I had just departed from. We sneaked onto the ferry—a very different ferry, as I recall, since the island was not yet the address it is now—and made it all the way to the island before a security guard noticed us trying to walk off the ferry by ourselves. We were taken to the resort and sat in the guard shack there for three hours while we waited for one of our parents to pick us back up after security finally managed to finagle our phone number out of Nate. We both prayed it would be our mother who'd show up, but it was dad who rolled up in our old Ford Fairmont station wagon. We could see him through the window, his face scraggly with a week's worth of beard, a Marlboro dangling between his lips, his eyes covered by those narrow black Ray-Ban sunglasses he used to wear, even though it was near dusk by then. He didn't bother to turn the car off and come inside the shack; he just leaned on the horn.

"That your pop?" the guard asked. When neither of us answered, he sighed deeply and opened the door. I don't remember if the guard seemed pained by the experience, embarrassed or just happy we were leaving, though I'd like to think it was pain I heard in the sigh. "Well, get on, then," he said and we did. I expected Dad would snap at us or take a swipe at our heads, but he just drove home in stony silence the entire way, chain-smoking and listening to talk radio, which was even more upsetting. It was predictable that he'd blow. This new quiet was something larger and somehow more aggressive, so that when we got home and found our bedrooms trashed, the posters torn off our walls, our beds turned upside down, *Star Wars* action figures and GI Joes tossed about, it all made sense and made me happy we'd sneaked out to this odd piece of paradise, if only to save ourselves from something that was apparently far worse.

"Here we are," Sam said. We'd pulled up in front of a two-story cream-colored compound. As we made our way onto the property, I put down the windows in the Cadillac and inhaled deeply to erase the old memories and to get acclimated to the new situation. The house was surrounded by a dozen swaying palms and row after row of three-foot-tall rosebushes that sprinkled the light breeze coming in off Biscayne with a sweet, florid fragrance, but I noted that they were in desperate need of trimming. I turned and looked behind me and saw that the box hedges lining the front of the drive were more like dodecahedron hedges. There was an acre-wide expanse of lawn along the eastern side of the house; it was also overgrown. Clouds of aphids could be seen here and there, as well, moving about in the humid afternoon.

In front of the house was a circular drive around a tasteful marble fountain, the water blooming out from the center and falling down like strands of hair. The house itself was a testament to natural light, with huge picture windows dominating the face of the home and wrapping around the length of the residence, the ocean visible even from the front yard.

Clarity on my creeping nontopiary suspicions came when I stepped out of the car and noticed a sign plastered to the garage door of the home, its corners reinforced with duct tape, announcing a public auction of the property and its contents in ten days' time.

"You didn't mention this," I said, pointing to the sign.

"Are you looking to move?" Sam said.

"It speaks to a certain amount of emotional and economic instability," I said.

"I said she was difficult," Sam said.

Before I could respond, the front door opened and a woman in her early fifties stepped out onto the front porch. Cricket O'Connor was tall, maybe five foot eight, and had shoulder-length blond hair, which she nervously tucked behind both of her ears when she saw us standing on her drive. I hoped she hadn't heard our conversation, but it was quickly apparent she had.

"I've tried to take the notice down," Cricket said. There was an absent, resigned quality to her voice, which belied her confident demeanor. She was dressed in a yellow St. John knit sweater set that revealed a tan expanse of neck and a thin gold necklace bedazzled with diamonds. A matching bracelet was wrapped around her left wrist. She wore a single diamond ring on her wedding finger and what looked liked a charm bracelet that dangled a single item on her right wrist. "But it's apparently against the law. Someone drives by every couple days to make sure it's still there, and if it's down, they put another up. It's not as invasive as the people who come to take photos, so I've learned to live with smaller inconveniences, even if it speaks to a larger instability."

"That's all anyone can be expected to do," I said. I walked over and extended my hand. "I'm Michael Westen. You have a lovely home."

Cricket forced a smile, shook my hand gingerly and then toyed with her single charm, which I saw was actually a military dog tag, before responding. "Well, for now at least. Please come in."

The difference between trained liars and your

garden-variety fibbers is that specific training allows for certain insights into the human condition not normally acquired while playing shell games on the pier or trying to con your waitress out of more change. At the (grateful) expense of the American tax payer, you're taught to look for signals of weakness so that whatever your particular cover might be or whatever your particular lie is eventually targeted to mete out can have its most effective power.

But sometimes, all you need to do is listen to someone talk and you can work out the subtext of their lives without once checking for the slight rise of red into their neck when they're sad, the sweat that appears first along the hairline when the first hint of stress appears or the involuntary reflexive shift when your intestines pick up the speed of fear.

Sam and I sat beside each other on a down-filled sofa in the middle of what was probably once a very well-appointed living room, but now looked a lot like an empty living room, save for an antique coffee table covered with old issues of *Architectural Digest*, including one that featured on the cover the very house we were sitting in, and an ottoman missing its chair. Across from us was a marble-lined fireplace with an elaborate mantel covered in framed photos of two men, one old and one young. The older man was pictured aboard a yacht in one photo, in black tie in another and with his arms around a much younger Cricket in yet another. The young man was pictured as a toddler, as a teen and as a Marine.

Over a dozen other framed items lay beneath one of the picture windows atop a white sheet.

Cricket stepped into the room and set a platter of cheese and crackers on the coffee table and then sort of stared at us, like she wasn't sure what she was supposed to do, which was probably the case.

"Sam tells me you have a problem," I said, because I was already starting to feel depressed about this whole situation that was about to be presented and I didn't even know what it was. Something about a six-million-dollar home up for auction and suspiciously missing most of its furniture tends to get me down. Plus, I had the general sense that every moment I wasn't figuring out the Natalya situation was another moment the target on my back got a little larger.

Cricket sat down on the ottoman and stifled a laugh as she sunk into it. "Do you know what this ottoman is worth?"

Sam leaned forward and touched the fabric. "What do you call that?"

"Chenille," she said.

"Very nice," he said. "I'd say a grand."

"I think it was a rhetorical question," I said.

"No," she said, "I'm done with rhetorical questions. I'm hoping to just get a decent appraisal. You two seem just as qualified as anyone else. Everyone seems to want a little less for good work these days."

"Looks like fine Italian craftsmanship to me," Sam said. "I'd give you fifteen hundred dollars for it."

"Sold," she said. "I'll take cash."

"I'm a little short," Sam said, and the way things were going, it didn't seem like this was going to be one of those jobs that would change my financial profile, either.

"Yes, well," she said and then made a sweep of her hand across the room and her eyes started to well up.

Crying women have never been my forte, nor furniture, so I said, "Cricket, I don't mean to be rude here, and I appreciate the cheese and crackers and the emotional vulnerability, but could we jump to the part where you just start talking about things directly? I'm sort of a no-metaphor guy."

Sam shot me a look that I ignored. It was probably meant to convey disappointment.

"I'm sorry, but this is all very embarrassing. I don't know where to start."

"Why not try the beginning?" I said. "But skip over the bits you don't think I'll care about."

Cricket smoothed out an imaginary wrinkle on her shirt and smiled faintly at me, which made me feel bad about being short, but the problem with most people is that they could work out most of their problems if they didn't spend so much time qualifying their lives. Give me an assignment, let me fix it and we'll go from there.

"My late husband, Scott O'Connor," Cricket said, pointing to the older man in the photos, "was a very wealthy man, but not an exceptionally good man, I'm afraid. He bought and sold companies for a living, just like his father had done, and his grandfather, too. I was under the impression that we had a very strong marriage, that I was the love of his life and that he cherished our son above all things. When he died from a heart attack a little over ten years ago, I learned that he had other women—an uncountable number, it would turn out—and other children, at least nine, though that number tends to fluctuate depending upon the month and the lawsuit. So what was once a great amount of money was significantly less, but more than enough, certainly. Nevertheless, I've spent the better part of the last decade giving away most of the money to charities throughout Miami, trying, not so vainly, to undo some of what I think of as my husband's least admirable traits."

Cricket stood up then and went across the room, picked up a few of the framed items from the sheet and handed them to me. They were certificates of appreciation from organizations like the South Beach AIDS Project, the Homeless Fund and the American Cancer Society.

"You've done good work," I said.

There were also photos of her cozied up with numerous celebrities, including a few fellows who ran for president over the years. In some of the photos, it was hard to tell if she was out on a date and was caught by paparazzi or if she actually was doing good work, though everyone gets to make their own choices about what is and isn't work these days.

"I've tried," Cricket said. "I hate who I found out my husband was, but I still love Scott, the man I was married to, the boy I met in college. I've tried to honor that original emotion, but then everything got fouled up." She went on to explain that her son, Devin, enlisted in the Marines after September eleventh, despite being in his second year at Princeton. "It was foolish," she continued. "I tried to dissuade him from it but he said that he felt useless, that college wasn't for him, which it wasn't. He took that from me, I suppose. But he went and I'm happy to say he was a fine soldier, that he loved what he was doing." Her voice trailed off then into silence.

"I was in Iraq for a little while," I said. "Anyone who went there, who lived even a day, is a better man than anyone walking on South Beach."

"Still," she said, "I'd prefer he was alive."

"How long has it been?" Sam asked.

"Two years last month," she said. Cricket started pacing the length of the room, her story flowing out of her like an avalanche of utter personal misery. It was after Devin died that things really fell apart for Cricket O'Connor, if it's possible to have your life fall apart even more than finding out the man you loved happened to love several other women and a baseball team of children. At first, she was feted in the local press, a minor celebrity for the fact that her son had perished, that her son had even enlisted in the first place, since rare is the warrior who comes from grace, and grace is something Cricket O'Connor possessed in spades. Benefit after benefit called upon Cricket O'Connor to be the face of their own grief and she just kept saying yes, giving money and time and press. And then there were the dates with celebrities.

Meetings with politicians.

A place in society.

Her hair perfect.

Her clothes designer.

Her jewels sparkling on the pages of *Haute Living*, the society column of the *Miami Herald* following her every date, *South Beach* naming her the most eligible woman in the city, and the most giving. *Palm Life* naming her one of their Fifty Most Beautiful Under Sixty.

"And then I met Dixon Woods," she said.

"Why do I know that name?" I asked.

"He did a little Special Forces time," Sam said. "The Tupac Amaru action in Panama?"

"I wasn't there," I said. "Not technically."

"Neither was he," Sam said. "Not technically. Buddy of mine in the NSA says he was also not technically in Nicaragua, Haiti and Bakino Faso, but that he's technically been in private service since 2002."

Just like every gun with a debt margin they want to work down, though I had a difficult time imagining anyone who'd done the things Dixon Woods was likely to have done somehow ending up in the arms of Cricket O'Connor. I had sensed the difficult part of Cricket O'Connor's life story was just now unfolding.

That and Sam was sort of twitching in his seat.

"Just how did you end up meeting Dixon Woods?" I said.

"On the Internet," she said.

"Pardon me?" I said.

"I'm part of several online support groups for relatives of military dead. One of them is also for singles. He contacted me there."

I already knew where this was headed. The world was simpler when people actually met each other in real life. The old model of getting drunk, dancing and doing things you regretted was a good one.

"You married him and he stole your money."

The color drained from Cricket's face. "How did you know?"

"Because predators can smell the weak even through a computer screen." What I didn't tell her: Because if I'd lived a second longer with my father, if I hadn't gone into the military after high school, I'd probably be doing the same thing as Dixon Woods.

A bully can always find a victim.

"I hate to be a cliché," she said.

"You're not," I said. "You're a foregone conclusion. That's worse, I'm sorry to say. But you don't need me to tell you that."

"That's why I need your help," Cricket said. "I needed someone to tell me that, obviously, and I need someone to help me find Dixon before I lose everything."

Need. Everyone thinks they *need* something. What Cricket O'Connor was really talking about was *want*: She wanted me to solve her problems, to fix what she'd wrecked with her own *needs*.

"I'm sorry your husband was a scumbag. I'm sorry

your son is dead. I'm even sorry you married someone you met on the Internet. But you need to call the police. Let them handle this."

"I can't do that," she said.

"Sure you can," I said. "Dial nine-one-one. They'll ask you if this is an emergency. Say yes. Go from there."

"Sam said you'd be able to help find Dixon," she said.

"Really?" I said to Sam.

"Mikey," he said, "there're some mitigating circumstances that don't exactly scream for proper law enforcement involvement."

"Is this where the *sort-of* drug dealers come in, or did I miss that part?"

"That would indeed be this part, yes," Sam said.

Cricket explained that the last time she saw Dixon he informed her that he needed a substantial amount of money to pay off a debt to opium dealers he was "engaged with in Afghanistan," where, he told her, he was working under contract with a private security firm, overseeing "certain American interests" in the opium trade. As soon as he got back from the job, he'd be reimbursed and she'd be reimbursed.

"And there'd be a little something on the back end for you, too, right?"

"Yes," Cricket said.

"How much?"

"I don't know. A couple hundred thousand. Maybe less."

"For a rich person," I said, "you sure are greedy."

Cricket began to well up, and I decided that, no

matter what was going on with this woman, I was having a hard time feeling any sympathy for her. You feel like you can run with wolves, every now and then you have to expect to get bitten.

"What do you take me for, Mr. Westen?" she asked, her voice just a whisper.

"The truth?"

"It would be refreshing these days."

I told her. And then I told her if there was nothing else, we'd be on our way.

"Wait here for just a moment," she said. She left the living room and made her way upstairs. I could hear her moving from room to room, opening and closing drawers.

Sam stood up, stretched and then went over to the mantel and picked up one of the photos of Devin, the Marine. "Remember when you enlisted?"

"Best day of my life," I said. "Of the seventy-five hundred subsequently, this one is near the bottom."

"She's a complicated woman," Sam said.

"She's a socialite with a champagne problem," I said. Sam handed me the photo of Cricket's son. When I was a kid, I always thought of Marines as men, but those old John Wayne movies lied. Back before the war, you enlisted and the oldest guy you were likely to run into in your battalion would be twenty-five. Devin O'Connor didn't look old enough to change the oil in a car, much less drive a Bradley. When you're twenty, you think it will all last forever. And how long was forever these days? A month, the girl at the Oro told me.

I handed Sam the photo back just as Cricket was coming back down the stairs. In her hands was a stack of cards, letters, photos.

"Cricket," I said, "I understand: You give away a lot of money to big corporate diseases and you sleep with celebrities who give even more money and that you're very, very important and . . ."

Before I could continue, Cricket dropped the bundle on the coffee table and I saw that these were different kinds of photos. Men—boys—with missing arms, legs, feet, eyes were smiling up in photos. Entire families. I sifted through the letters. Some were those annoying Christmas rundowns on fancy printed paper, others were handwritten in crayon. Some were Hallmark cards that inside simply said *thank you* a hundred times. Pictures of babies. "What is this?" I asked.

"The day Devin was killed," she said, "he was on a mission in Tikrit. He and fifteen other boys were going house to house looking for weapons. Suffice to say, they found some. Seven of those boys died, the rest suffered horrible, horrible injuries. I've been using whatever resources I have to take care of those families. Most of them have nothing, you know, just what the government gives them. So I've paid for what I can. Pyschiatric care. Car payments. Mortgages. Whatever they have asked for, I have been happy to help with. And you know what the funny thing is, Mr. Westen?"

I couldn't think of anything funny.

"They hardly ever ask. So I ask them. Every night.

I send out a hundred e-mails, probably, to these poor boys and their families, and I ask what they need. And they need so much, but they so rarely feel like they should. That's what I was using that money for, Mr. Westen. That's what I have stopped doing these last few weeks. That is what I must do. Do you understand?"

"I do," I said. I did. I really did. Cricket O'Connor smelled like a victim and that was a shame.

"I may be stupid, but I'm not evil. I'm trying to do good things. I'm trying to give someone the same opportunities my son had. I'm trying to help people. I thought this money was legitimate. I thought Dixon was legitimate."

"Okay," I said. "Okay. I get it. Now, when did the drug dealers start threatening to kill you?"

"Why would you think that?"

"Experience. Intuition. The very fact that Sam has me sitting here with you in the first place when I could be at home doing sit-ups."

Cricket looked over at Sam, who just shrugged. He looked smart in his sport coat, which probably made her think he was the brains in the operation and I was the muscle, or at least she figured Sam understood her better since he was sleeping with Veronica. "Just after Dixon left for Afghanistan again," she said. First, she told us, it was just a series of phone calls asking for Dixon and when she told the callers that Dixon was gone, wouldn't be back for months, that if they had a problem they should contact Longstreet, the security firm he was employed by. This was met by laughter, which she found disconcerting. By the last phone call, her responses were met with simple threats upon Dixon's person. It was a few days later that she noticed the same boat circling past her property over and over again. And then, finally, the knock on her front door.

At three a.m.

When she opened the door, there were three men standing there with guns.

"Dixon told me that there might be trouble one day," she said. "But I didn't expect this."

"Really," I said. "Pretty prescient on his part." There was nothing about Dixon Woods, at least in Cricket's description, that made me think he was anything like a Special Forces guy. Guys like Dixon Woods, if he thought his wife was in danger, would have guys like me, or guys like Sam, waiting for the trouble and in a place to defuse it.

"He said that in his line of work, sometimes people got angry. That for my own safety, it might be important for us to assume new identities, things like that."

"And that wasn't a red flag, Cricket?" Sam said. His voice was plenty calm because he was trying to sound sensitive, I suspect, but I also think he couldn't believe what he was hearing now, either.

"I thought it was exciting. I thought it would be an adventure. I haven't been a happy person and this offered me a release. Neither of you are women. You don't know what it feels like to be with a person who is dangerous. It's exhilarating."

The funny thing was, I did know what she was

talking about. Fiona and I had once had the very same conversation. At least Fiona knows how to handle herself. "Who did you think you were going to be," I said, "Nick and Nora Charles?"

"I didn't think at all," she said.

The men came inside, searched the house for Dixon, sat down where Sam and I were sitting at that moment and gave her a very clear ultimatum: They'd like their money back. Now. She gave them what she had on her—a few thousand dollars—and then they began taking things like jewels and furniture.

"Back up," I said. "When was the last time you saw Dixon?"

"It's been almost three months," she said. "He was in Afghanistan for a few weeks, came home and then left again."

"Uh-huh," I said. "This Dixon, what's his waist size?"

"Like on a pair of pants?"

"Exactly."

"Well," she said, "I'm not sure."

You want to know how well a woman knows her husband, ask her the size of his pants. You want to know how well a woman doesn't know her husband, ask her the same question. I knew the answer to the next question, but I asked it anyway. "Do you have a picture of him, Cricket?"

"No," she said, "he never allowed that. He said it was a security issue."

"Of course he did," I said. "Did he ever refer to

himself as a spook?" Cricket reached for her neck and I actually heard Sam give out a little groan. I took that as an affirmative. "And how long have you been married?"

"A year."

"And how much money did he need?" I asked.

"The last time?"

"God, yes, the *last time*," I said.

"A million dollars," she said.

"And you just cut a check?"

"He's my husband," she said.

"And how much did the bad guys want?"

"Two million dollars," she said.

"And you cut another check?"

"No," she said. "I took equity from my home. And then they came back. And then they came back again. They keep coming back asking for more and more money, or they'll kill me and kill Dixon, as soon as they find him. And now, well, now I'm going to lose everything and so will those families, Mr. Westen."

"Okay," I said, "but tell me you're not doing this for Dixon, too."

"He's my husband," Cricket said again.

"Probably not," I said.

And that was when the tears really came. It might have been smart to get Fiona involved in this situation ahead of time, since, when she wants to, she can provide feminine comfort and that sort of thing. But instead it was me and Sam watching this put-together woman of means break down into sobs. Sam got up and guided her back over to the ottoman, sat down beside her, patted her knee, told her to settle down, that we'd get through this together and that we'd get the bad guys who were putting her through all of this, though I didn't really have any concept of who the bad guys actually were or what *this* was. I got the Dixon Woods part, but I didn't see who else was involved. I figured Sam didn't either, but that Cricket was one of Veronica's friends and he needed to be sensitive to that.

Or, like me, the crying was starting to make him frantic.

What I'd figured out and would have happily elucidated to Cricket was that it was highly unlikely Dixon Woods was anywhere near Afghanistan. I would have also told her that she'd probably been scammed out of her money (and I didn't know yet how much money in total that equaled) and that she was better off looking into a trade of some kind, or maybe dialing up one of the famous people whose arm she'd found herself on when she had money and asking them for a small loan to get out of town with. I might have also told her that I had real doubts that Dixon Woods was actually Dixon Woods, but then Cricket blew her nose, dabbed her eyes and thanked Sam for his kindness.

And just like that, Cricket O'Connor was perfectly composed again. There was something about Cricket O'Connor that I found troubling: how a person who seemed so capable of handling life could be so incapable of seeing how much she was risking before it actually happened.

It reminded me of Natalya.

"You'll have to pardon me," she said. "I understand, Mr. Westen, that you think I'm a fool, but I wonder if you've ever found yourself in a situation beyond your control."

If she only knew. "There've been occasions."

"I fell in love with Dixon," she said. "That was probably a mistake. We don't always make the right choices in whom we love, but I believed in him and I believed him when he told me he'd been in the Special Forces and I believed him when he told me he was providing private security in Afghanistan and I believed him when he told me he was in trouble and desperately needed my help. And I believed the men who came to my home and threatened to kill me if I didn't turn Dixon in. I loved him, Mr. Westen. I *love* him. Maybe people like you and people like Dixon can just turn real emotion on and off, but for the rest of the human race, things are a bit more trying." She paused then and tried to smile, as if changing her facial expression could change the outcome of all that had come before. "And I believed Sam when he said you would help me. If I go to the police, these men will find Dixon and they will kill him. And I know they will kill me. And . . . " She paused again. "I don't want this to be in the paper. As soon as the police know about this, it will be all over the papers. I'll be a mockery. I have nowhere else to turn. I can't pay you much, but whatever I can give you, I will. Please, Mr. Westen."

"These bad guys," I said, "they give you a way to

contact them? A drop zone for the money? Anything?"

"They gave me a cell phone," she said.

"Go get it," I said.

A few moments later, Cricket came back with a burner, a prepaid cell you can get in any half-assed check-cashing front shop in Little Haiti or the nicest sundry shop on South Beach. Used to be only drug dealers and sixteen-year-old girls whose mothers didn't trust them not to abuse their minutes had burners. Now, half the world. They're impossible to get a wire on because once you're up on them, they're already dead.

"They call on this, make sure I'm home, then come for the cash," she said.

"When are they due to call again?"

"Thursday. The fifteenth. It's always the fifteenth."

"Pay day," Sam said.

"Not anymore," I said.

"So you're going to help me?" Cricket said.

When you're a spy, or a former one, or just one trying to figure out how your life got turned upside down by someone else's choices, someone else's agenda, someone else's ego and hubris and wanton disregard for who you are as a human, sometimes, well, a soft spot opens up for people in a similar situation.

"I'm going to get your money back," I said, "as much as I can. Enough for you to live. To help the other people. But you have to listen to me. You have to do as I tell you to do. And you have to understand one thing."

"Anything," she said.

"You're not married to Dixon Woods," I said. "You've probably never met him. This guy you're not married to is a criminal, and he's gaming you. When I find him, after I get your money, he's likely going to be hurt. He might be dead. He might well be going to prison. And this house? This lifestyle? It's over. It's not yours. You want to help people. To really help people? I'll get that back for you if I can."

Cricket closed her eyes. Her head moved slightly in agreement.

"Why don't you go upstairs and pack a bag?" I said. "Sam will come back later and take you somewhere safe."

Sam and I watched Cricket mount the stairs toward her bedroom and then, when we heard the sobbing begin, let ourselves out of the house.

"Nice speech," Sam said once we were outside.

"These people," I said, "don't know how lucky they have it."

"Yeah," Sam said. "Still. Quite a bit of oration there."

I put on my sunglasses and walked back along the side of Cricket's house. From there I could see Biscayne Bay, full this day with sail boats and yachts lazing back and forth through the shipping lanes. Sam came and stood beside me. "Nice view," I said.

"If you like this sort of thing," Sam said.

"I could get on a boat from here," I said. "Sail all the way up the Eastern Seaboard. Park in New York. Hop on a train, be in Washington D.C. in no time. Start pounding on doors. Who'd ever know?"

"I would," Sam said.

"Or I could just go due south. Find a sandbar and call it home. Forget this burn notice and everything else."

"Ah, Mikey, that's not your life," Sam said.

And the truth, the sad truth, was that he was right.

4

There's nothing easy about having a lot of actual cash money, particularly if your job description is something other than armored-car driver. If you sell drugs, extort cash from socialites or happen to be running an international cartel funded by Colombians and protected by Russians, or just happen to be a grifter with a way with women, you still need to find a place to keep your money other than the bank, because a million actual dollars weigh a ton. Literally. You get a million dollar bills, they will weigh a ton. You get your million dollars broken down into hundreds, it's only twenty pounds.

You still need to find a way to pay your bills. So you have to clean that money, get it into the system so that you can live.

Because even if you're a malicious crime lord or evil genius, you probably still have cable, water, power and HOA fees to take care of at your secret hideout, which, usually, is just a very large home in a master-planned community since underground lairs, hollowed-out volcanoes and bases on the dark side of the moon have become harder and harder to come by. But beyond that, if someone hands you a check for a million dollars, you can't just deposit it and you can't just cash it.

Fortunately, Miami is only a puddle jumper away from the Caribbean, where illegal banking is practically a spectator sport. Or, if you're really industrious, you can go on a run from the Caribbean down to Guyana, where money laundering and the drug trade make up a sum close to fifty percent of the country's economy. So if you're a drug dealer, have a few million dollars in American cash and the ability to set up a nice shelter corporation—say, a timber company, which in Guyana is the favored business of drug dealers looking to get legit return on their dollars—and have a fast boat, or a decent plane, or enough contacts, you can do just about anything to get your money back into the U.S. in a way that it comes back smelling like Tide.

I had a pretty good idea that the money being moved around the perimeter of Cricket O'Connor's life was being cleaned by someone, somewhere. First rule of dealing with assholes: Follow the money.

"When I was robbing banks for the IRA, it wasn't so difficult to move money," Fiona said. I'd gone to her condo in the marina after meeting with Cricket, and Sam went off to do a little snooping. I filled Fiona in on the details, plus some of my suspicions, and then sat at her kitchen table and thumbed through a stack of society magazines that Cricket O'Connor had given me earlier in the day, hoping to catch a glimpse of the man she called Dixon Woods in the background of someone else's photo spread, since she told me the two of them had "made the scene" whenever he was in town. The "scene" looked to be something like the senior prom, but with elaborate ice sculptures instead of balloon art and no one under fifty-five to be found, but in pretty much the same gaudy outfits.

While Fiona cooked a Persian dish that had a lot of onions, peppers and lamb in it, and that smelled vaguely like the month I spent living above a café in Iran a few years back, I also tried to figure out how to approach the whole Natalya issue. I hadn't told Fiona about Natalya yet, knowing that it would be the sort of thing that would probably cause her to purchase guns for her own personal use, and I wanted to control that situation for as long as I could.

"You walked in," Fiona continued, her voice downright wistful, "shot a few people in the knees, locked a few others in the vault and then took what you needed. You drove down the street, ran up the stairs of the flat, dumped the money out on the bed, rolled around a bit and then went out for a pint."

"A simpler time," I said. The magazine I was reading—and by reading, I mean flipping through with a growing unease—was something called *Palm Life*, a magazine dedicated to, according to the slug line on its masthead, "the good life and golden years beneath the palms." There weren't any actual stories in the magazine, just elaborate photo spreads with a descriptive paragraph about who was in the picture and why those people were, I guess, living the good life beneath the palms. "Tell me something, Fi. What is the allure of being seventy and wearing a tiger-print miniskirt?"

"Being trashy isn't just for young women anymore, Michael," she said. Fiona set a plate of sizzling vegetables and meat in front of me and took the magazine from my hands. "You could do quite well in this world. Find yourself a refurbished wife and just stand by her side while she gets her picture taken. You'd need a better tan, though. And a pair of yellow pants wouldn't hurt, apparently."

"If that's the good life, I'll stick with whatever this is."

"It's funny how none of these women have any wrinkles," she said, flipping the pages.

"None that you can see." I ate a few bites of the dish. It was surprisingly tasty. "When did you become such a good cook?"

"Your mother and I are taking an online cooking class together," she said. She'd stopped on a double-page spread of a pool party at some mansion. There were men in Speedos who would have been better off in girdles.

"When I was a kid," I said, "if it wasn't made from a box of macaroni and cheese or wasn't served in a tin foil dish courtesy of Swanson's, it wasn't homemade."

"You're a little old to be blaming your bad childhood for anything," she said. "At least not anything you've done since you met me."

Fiona was probably right. But I'd learned plenty about being a spy by being a kid. First improvised-explosive device I ever made was in the backyard of a neighbor's house after Nate and I were kicked out one evening for complaining about the culinary options. You want to blow something up but are afraid you just don't have the skill set? Go into your garage, grab some disinfectant. Better: If you live in a place like Miami, you probably have a high-grade pool cleaner, but even if you don't, your local home-improvement store does. Buy a gallon. Grab some liquid soap.

Mix them together.

Stand back.

You're done.

Potassium permanganate and glycerin: best friends for young arsonists and prospective spies alike. You have children and want to get their attention away from their iPods, video games and the Internet? Teach them to blow things up.

We saw our dad create that particular explosive concoction in the garage one afternoon by accident. It's one of my few good memories of him. Anyway, it taught me how to make things go bang during a bad situation.

Which got me thinking about Dixon Woods again. I had to figure out a way to draw him out, get close enough to him to figure out where the money was, or where it had gone, and why he needed it in the first place. I figured if he just wanted a quick score, he could have had one. Coming back for more, getting married, all that—it screamed of intricacy. Greed was one thing. But this kind of personal involvement was something different.

"You say you're doing something online with my mother?" I said.

"Online. Offline. We are getting very close." Fiona was already working through another issue of *Palm Life*, this one with a picture of Priscilla Presley gracing the cover. She sat on the hood of a Bentley beneath a headline trumpeting a charity called "Hound Dogs for Humanity." Fiona flipped a page and I saw her eyebrows rise in actual surprise, rare coming from Fiona. She slid the magazine over to me. "How do you dance when you're hooked to an oxygen tank?"

"Slowly," I said. In the foreground of the photo, a man in pink gabardine slacks and matching liver spots was doing a kind of palsied shimmy alongside his tank and a girl—she wasn't a woman, at least not in the conventional sense, particularly since her most prominent parts didn't look much older than toddler age—in a tight black dress and about a quarter million dollars in diamonds.

But that wasn't what Fi was surprised by. In the background of the picture was a woman who looked a lot like Cricket O'Connor doing a shimmy of her own, but the man she was dancing with was blurred by movement. The paragraph beneath the photo indicated that it was taken during a fund-raiser for literacy . . . held at a nightclub called Love/Blue. Not a lot of things that happen in Miami make sense when you look at them directly. A benefit for literacy at a nightclub didn't even register on my egregiousness barometer. But the picture was a nice reminder: Scan the background, dig a little, you'll find the dirt you expected.

In this case, there were likely hundreds of shots taken at this event—probably two dozen of this one moment alone, particularly if the photographer had a sense of humor—and that meant there was a strong likelihood a photo of Dixon Woods, whoever he really was, would be in one of them and we'd be able to start making good on one of my core beliefs: that people frequently do illegal things out of desperation and stupidity. It was clear Dixon was desperate for money—and that whoever he'd screwed was desperate to get their money back, too—but it was also clear Dixon was stupid in a very basic way: He made poor, sloppy decisions, and that meant he was probably already juicing someone else like he had juiced Cricket, or was about to.

Figuring out what the hell he looked like would be a good start. Cricket's description of him—"tall, wavy brown hair, brown eyes, a little thick in the middle, a very hairy chest and a body like Sam's"—boiled him down to about three billion men. Not a good statistical control.

Nevertheless, Sam was going to spend the afternoon checking a bit more deeply into Dixon, though we both knew that it was unlikely to lead us anywhere directly related to Cricket's problem. We also knew that to know Dixon Woods' name in the first place meant that whoever was pulling this grift knew more than he should.

It was a level of the game we didn't impart to Cricket. I figured it could wait. First, we had to figure out who we were dealing with. I told Fiona that I thought it would be nice if she used her online time—in between her Learning Annex classes with Mom—to create an enticing profile on one of the singles support groups Cricket had originally used, a plan she immediately embraced.

"Maybe I'll get a bit of an eyebrow lift, too," she said.

We'd need to see about a photo, no matter what. The offices of *Palm Life* might turn up the evidence Cricket couldn't. Predictably, according to the masthead, the offices for *Palm Life*, which covered the good life of the golden years under the palms, were located in a fashionable neighborhood of Coral Gables, a good dozen miles from even a marginal life. I made a bet with Fiona that the offices would be surrounded by palm trees that not a single drunken couple had managed to desecrate and that they'd be happy palms, unlike the ones near my mother's house, which have that sad, dead look caused by too many fruit rats using them as their winter homes.

I checked my watch. It was just past noon. Plenty of time to play dress-up with the media folks.

"You feel like going on a field trip?" I asked.

"Depends," she said. "Are we stopping by the Hotel Oro first to exact some bloody revenge?"

I figured I had two choices here. Tell the truth or lie. The problem in dealing with Fiona is that either response was likely to end up with violence. Fiona didn't think fondly of Natalya, to say the least. She never really appreciated knowing anything about anyone I'd ever been with who wasn't her; tended to react poorly upon meeting these women, tended to react with escalating anger, then violence, then protracted gun battles and high-powered explosives. Best-case scenarios involved the pulling of hair.

Gut punches performed with brass knuckles.

Car bombs.

Certain treaties being revoked.

This situation? The threats against her? The threats against me? Well, that was the sort of deal that would take some massaging, particularly if I wanted her to help me, which I would. Eventually. Not quite yet. But soon.

"That turned out to be nothing," I said.

"Did you know that I have perfected the Palestinian hanging technique?"

I took a bite of lamb and peppers, and chewed thoughtfully. "This really is excellent."

"What is so interesting is that you don't even really hang. It's more like death by crucifixion, minus all of that awful martyrdom. A slow, excruciating death." Fiona took the fork out of my hand, stabbed a chunk of gristle that I'd pushed to one side of the plate, and then ate it, smiling all the while. "This is lovely. You're right."

"Fi . . ." I said.

"Of course," she said, "I've been reading quite a bit about this new torture technique they're testing now in Pakistan. It's really very revolutionary. You take a conventional hot box and you throw in a live electrical wire. As the humidity in the room rises from the prisoner's labored breathing, the air actually turns electric. Like a lightning storm in a room. Only done it on rats thus far, but I'd be willing to bet that a human would make it work spectacularly."

"Fi," I said, "listen. I handled the situation. Everything is going to be fine. A little issue of mistaken identity. But I cleared it up and everyone involved is sorry that you were ever in jeopardy. They'd even like to buy the guns."

"That's so sweet," she said. She reached over and touched my cheek and I thought, *Huh, I didn't think that was going to work. Especially that part about the guns. That was a real stretch. How am I going to make good on that?* And then I realized that the touch Fiona was giving me was actually gaining in intensity, that she was now actually gripping my face, was digging her thumb into my jaw. Was sort of affecting my breathing.

"Fi," I said, but it came out sounding more like *flea* because my jaw wouldn't open and my tongue's movements were impeded.

"Natalya Choplyn? Really, Michael? You're lying to me about her *again*? I have to hear it from *Sam?*"

I liked it better when Fiona and Sam didn't get along, kept secrets from each other, used me only as a sounding board for complaints and threats. For the better part of a decade, it was one of those points I knew would remain fixed. For the first month I was back home, I was fairly certain Fiona would shoot Sam, provided Sam didn't dime her to one agency or another, foreign or domestic. There was an incident several years ago—money was lost, bullets were fired, flesh wounds were had—that left both feeling, well, *distrustful* of each other.

Things have changed.

Having them in cahoots makes things far less predictable, far more personally painful, at least as this situation started to present itself.

I could have just grabbed Fiona's arm and flipped her over her chair, pinned her to the ground, put an elbow to her throat and told her to believe me, but I didn't have time to have an entire afternoon of acrobatic, angry, vengeful sex with Fiona. Not that I didn't want to. Not that I probably didn't need to. But that I couldn't. Vows have been made: *Keep things less personal. More professional. The fewer nude exchanges the better.* I knew better than to engage Fiona physically. It never ended well emotionally and I've been trying to be more neutral there.

Search for ennui.

Find inertia.

Avoid foreplay at all costs. And fighting with Fiona was better than a dozen roses, diamond earrings and a steak dinner combined.

"I was going to tell you," I said. It came out sounding a lot like *I was going to kill you*, so Fiona let go of my face. An expression of eager anticipation glossed over her. I swiveled my head around and reset my jaw. I have to admit, she did look pretty cute when she was ready to really hurt you. "First," I said, "I want to remind you that when Natalya and I had our . . . summit . . . you and I were not you and I. And that you and I are not you and I."

"Oh, yes, I recall," she said. "That was one of your sabbaticals." She picked up my plate of food, which I wasn't finished with, walked over to the sink and scraped it all into the garbage disposal.

"Fi, do you want to know what's going on, or do you want to fight about things that happened in the last century?"

"I'm listening," she said. "I am also passing judgment, but don't let that stop you from spinning your little yarn." I told her everything there was to know. I didn't even leave out the part where Natalya told me I was looking good . . . except I tweaked that a bit to say she'd just complimented me on my suit and asked where I got my sunglasses. All the while, Fiona kept her back to me and pretended to clean her kitchen. As I neared the conclusion, I saw that she'd actually taken out several guns and was lining them up in an orderly fashion aside the drain board. The way the sun cut through the windows in her place made them shine across the room, so that I was nearly blinded by Fiona's passive-aggressive nonchalance.

"What do you propose to do?" Fiona asked.

"Well, first thing, I guess I need to find out why someone in our government is trying to get the Russians to kill me or have me tried for treason, or just pegged as a drug kingpin, none of which seem like great outcomes. And then figure out how to get Natalya to accept that I haven't done what I'm accused of. And, then, if all else fails, see where to get my hands on whatever vig she's in for. Or . . . " I paused and thought about it. "Or I guess I figure out how to get rid of her."

This brightened Fiona's mood considerably. "Why don't we just jump to the last choice?"

I explained, again, to Fiona that this was a person with kids. With a husband. With a life. That I couldn't just leave a trail of bodies around me wherever I went. Plus, I had the impression that Natalya had . . . changed. At least incrementally. I told Fiona, "When I said *get rid of her*, I didn't mean via a bullet to the back of the head and then a watery grave."

"I envisioned a threshing machine. No bullet at all. Very little residual evidence."

The truth was that I was prepared to do what I had to if she came at me.

Or my family.

Or Sam.

Or Fiona . . . again.

"Let's see where the Gandhi approach takes us first."

"It's nice you could have such humanistic feelings for a person who would have had me killed had I not been ten times more intelligent than she is,"

Fiona said. "Does she still have that awful hair? I recall her having awful hair and a very sinewy body. Or at least that's how she looked through my rifle scope. Terrible hair and truly repugnant taste in men."

When you're planning to infiltrate a hostile environment, it's important to take into consideration important factors: topography, weather, special equipment needs, disposition of the enemy, need for air support. You want to know the mind-set of the people you'll be dealing with so that you won't be surprised by the choices in logic they make. You want to know how to escape if everything collapses.

You want to avoid Coral Gables.

Specifically, the Alhambra Plaza, home to a pink stone Hyatt Regency and a complex of high-end office spaces and busy courtyards designed to make you feel like you're in Italy on the muggiest day in history. Coral Gables was one of the first planned communities in Florida, which means there are plenty of places for tourists to walk around with wall-eyed wonder at the shops and restaurants, for college students from The U to ride their bikes drunkenly down the wide paseos, and for four-way stops that bottle traffic while drivers consult their maps. A simple clue: Home is to the north. When you hit Canada, stop.

Palm Life's offices occupied the top floor of the Alhambra Plaza and were a testament to the power of pink. Pink marble on the ground. Pink sofas and

chairs—all stuffed to the point of cotton explosion—
in the lobby. Pink roses in towering vases placed in
every corner. If I followed the receptionist home, I'm
sure she'd have a little pink house.

As it was, she was young, beautiful, lithe and
tanned to the point of crispness. I suspected that her
name was probably Star, too, and that if I looked
over her résumé it would indicate a booming career
updating her MySpace page and a degree in Face-
book. Unlike the reservation clerks at the Oro, the
receptionist here was actually allowed to sit behind
a desk, albeit one made of pink marble, too. There
were back issues of *Palm Life* fanned out around her,
but I noticed she had an issue of *US* open on her
lap. Didn't anyone read *Soldier of Fortune* anymore?

"Can I help you?" she asked. I noticed she had
her fingernail pierced. Very classy.

"Yes," I said. "I'm Jay Gatz and this is Daisy
Miller. We have an appointment with the photo editor concerning our upcoming charity event."

The receptionist raised her ears and eyebrows up
at the same time. I guess the look she was going for
was surprise followed by deep thought. It was a neat
trick. If only more cocker spaniels could do it, the
world would be a different, more introspective place.
"Why do I know your names?" she said to me.

"He's exceptionally rich, darling," Fiona said.
"He's in your magazine nearly every month. Maybe
you don't recognize him without his oxygen tank."

This seemed to satisfy the receptionist. She made
a few clicks on the computer and then picked up

her phone and called someone, presumably the photo editor. Before we'd left Fiona's, I'd checked the masthead and hadn't found a single person listed in that capacity. I figured, best-case scenario, we'd get an editorial assistant who'd just give me whatever I asked for. Worst-case scenario, Fiona would hold the entire place under siege, and I'd get whatever I asked for.

I was hoping for a little uncontested middle ground.

"Hi, James? I have Jay Gatz and"—the receptionist pulled the phone away from her mouth and whispered to Fiona—"I'm sorry. What was your name?"

"Daisy Miller," Fiona said. It didn't matter. The receptionist was already back on the phone.

"Someone here to see you about their charity event." The receptionist nodded, scribbled something down on a Post-it, made a *he's so crazy* face at Fiona, just two girlfriends sharing the moronic intricacies of the male sex with each other and then hung up. "James says he doesn't have you down in his Crack-Berry, but since it's you, Mr. Gatz, he's happy to get you in." She ripped off the Post-it and handed it to me. "That's Mr. Dimon's office number. His name isn't on the door yet."

"What happened to . . . ?" I began.

"Gunther? Bailed to a younger-skewing magazine in Dallas. Said that was going to be the next hot place. Lots of clubs and stuff. Did you know that Lindsay Lohan bought a place out there? It's about to jump off."

"Darling," Fiona said, "don't you own an oil field there?"

"Two," I said.

"Oil is cool," the receptionist said.

"Like black gold," I said.

The receptionist got up and walked us over to a twelve-foot-tall smoked-glass door and flashed an ID card to unlock it, then held it open as we walked past. Used to be the only places with decent security actually had something to protect. What were they protecting here? The good life?

"I just love your nails," Fiona said, tapping her finger on the ring dangling off the girl's right pinky. "That style is ready to jump off."

James Dimon's office was decorated in Bekins—boxes stacked up in every corner, a desk covered in packing popcorn—but the walls were covered in framed covers of *Palm Life*, some dating as far back as the eighties. The weird thing about the 1980s is that even though that's when I grew up, I don't actually remember everyone looking like they'd just been cut out of a Nagle painting. I also don't remember seeing so many people wearing shoulder pads. But there they were.

"You'll have to excuse the mess," James said. He'd taken a seat behind his desk in a leather chair that looked brand-new after he cleared a spot for Fiona and me on an equally pristine-looking sofa, but kept getting up and moving around. Less nervous twitch, more Red Bull. "I'm still unpacking. Crazy move. I'm going to get these photos down, too. We're really changing the whole image of the magazine. Embracing the now." He wore tight, narrow-legged jeans that had a strategic tear along the left hip that revealed a splash of too-white skin. Of all the things not to be pink. He had on a black-and-silver pinstriped shirt that was unbuttoned one button too low and revealed a clammy-looking chest completely devoid of hair. His office smelled like an eighth-grade dance: too much cologne, nebulous sexuality.

"Where are you down from?" I asked. I wasn't trying to sound like Jay Gatz, but it was working for me, so I figured I'd ride it. Plus, I've always wanted to use *down* in that way, but always felt like it wouldn't come off unless I had a sweater tied over my shoulders or a sailor's cap on my head.

"Across, technically," he said. "I was working for a magazine in LA LA Land. Thought I'd give the Right Coast a try." When he said *Right Coast*, he made an air-quote gesture with his fingers. "I had an offer to roll in"—air quote—"the Hampty Hamps. Another shot in"—air quote—"Hot Lanta. Had another chance to go to"—air quote—"Vegas, baby"— here he laughed, because that's what guys like James Dimon do: They laugh when they say *Vegas, baby*— "but in the end, it's all about South Beach. Being present in the moment."

I expected that, at any moment, he'd refer to New York as the Apple, Paris as the City of Light and Beirut as the Paris of the Middle East, and that he'd use air quotes each time. I also expected that if we somehow got back to his job in Los Angeles, he'd drop City of Angels and Tinseltown in the mix, as if La La wasn't enough. If he managed to work his way to Reno being the Biggest Little City in the World, I was going to throw him off the building.

"Yeah," I said. I had to gather myself a little. The air quotes had me dizzy. "Listen. Daisy and I appreciate your time. Gunther was always so helpful, and we've had such a great relationship with the magazine over the years, and so I hope you can do me the smallest favor."

"Mr. Gatz, I'm happy to do anything you need. It's just an honor to meet you. I'm a fan of all that you do," he said. "And even though we're changing the direction of the rag, we'll always have space for you and your—" James stopped midsentence, as if he wasn't quite sure where he was going in his conversation with me, which was possible, since he had already professed to being my fan. He looked at Fiona. He looked back at me. Had some cosmic convergence, continued on. "And your"—air quote— "lady"—air quote—"as long as I'm in charge of the art. Though, candidly, we're going to be moving more toward a photojournalism vibe . . . toward a feeling of . . ." He started searching for words again, but I was afraid he was only given to one cosmic convergence a day, my sense being that James Dimon only knew about a hundred, hundred and fifty independent words, and the rest were catchphrases.

"Being present in the moment?" Fiona suggested. James Dimon snapped. As in, he actually started snapping. "Yes! Yes! That certain pâté de foie gras you just can't find in other magazines out here. Gritty. Real. That's where I'm headed with *Palm*."

"Wonderful," I said. And I meant it, so I put air quotes around it, let James know we were of the same mind-set.

"Stunning," Fiona said.

Fiona turned and gave me a coy glance that, in the past, has meant that the fuse is lit and we have twenty seconds to get out of the building before it comes crashing down around us. I figured it was more of an interior fuse in this case, so I said, "Wonderful," again, because if James Dimon truly hated everything that had come before his arrival—and I suspected his stay would be short enough that he'd probably want to hold on to the boxes, lest he announce that anyone or anything else had a pâté de fois gras—he probably would have no problem whatsoever letting me look through the photos of Cricket O'Connor tripping the light fantastic for literacy. In fact, I suspected that if I said *tripping the light fantastic*, he'd start snapping again, which was something I wanted to avoid until I really needed it, as an idea was beginning to take shape in my mind about how I might use someone of James Dimon's particular . . . *skill* . . . down the line. If he wanted gritty, realistic, *present in the moment* shots of South Beach's glitterati, I thought there'd be some opportunities for us both to benefit. "About that favor, sport," I said.

"Anything, Mr. Gatz."

Once you've infiltrated a hostile enemy environment, the best way to find out if anyone cares about anything is to be as general as possible. Have specifics ready in case the conversation should devolve, but on the strong chance you're dealing with someone who clearly only has eyes for themselves— which, in the civil world (or the world not possessed by top secret documents, locations of missing nuclear warheads, stashes of drugs and guns) is the majority of the population—all you'll need is earnest banality rendered in the blandest colors.

"There was a benefit we attended last year; and Daisy just adored the ice sculpture. We were hoping we might take a look through your file photos, perhaps make a copy or two, so that Daisy can show it to an artist she has in mind for our own event." I reached over and put my hand on Fiona's, to let James know this was all her fault, that we were just two guys who knew that when our *ladies* wanted something, well, we did what we could.

"What was the gig?"

The gig. I wondered if I was on camera somewhere. "A fund-raiser for literacy held at Love/Blue," I said.

"Yeah, yeah," James said. "What month was that?"

"May," Fiona said.

"May, and they had an ice sculpture?" James said. He shook his head like he was trying to get water out of his ears. "Cuh-razy." James gave us both an incredulous smile.

"Tell you what," I said. I was pretty much done being Jay Gatz. "Why don't you go get that magazine, figure out where you keep the photos and maybe bring me and *my lady* a bottle of water?" A yogurt wouldn't hurt, but I figured I shouldn't push it. Not that James Dimon would feel the push. He wouldn't have known if I broke two of his ribs. He'd just keep on keeping on. I added, "Please," however, just to be cordial.

"Hey, *pas de probleme*, Mr. Gatz." James stepped outside his office for a moment and came back in with the issue in hand. A moment later, an assistant walked in with water for both of us. I wasn't thirsty, but I liked asking James to get us water. "Yeah, yeah," he said. He had the magazine open and was scanning each image, commenting page by page. "Lighting was all wrong. Can't tell if it was a party or a funeral. Too many saggy-baggies. Gunther, always an F-stop off."

"James," I said. "*Sport*. That favor. The pictures."

An hour and forty minutes later, we found what we were looking for. James Dimon was long gone, as even he had quickly tired of our patter as we sifted through the photos—I said *sport* at least twelve times, Fiona used *darling* as a verb, noun and adjective, sometimes in the same sentence—and left us in the art morgue after the first five minutes, saying he had to get back to the *renovation of the moment*. I told him I'd be in touch. Fiona kissed him on both cheeks. He sent in his assistant with coffee and even more bottled water. It was like being on vacation.

After searching through contact sheets and stills filled with photos of young women dancing with old men, old women dancing with young men, young men dancing with old men, and young men dancing with other young men, all in the name of literacy and, it appeared, very shiny clothing, we finally found a photo of Dixon Woods and Cricket O'Connor.

It wasn't from the original photo in the magazine that first drew us into the office of *Palm Life*, but one that was taken as the guests were first arriving at the event. There were actually four photos taken of the couple, all a millisecond apart. In the first photo, Cricket and Dixon can be seen holding hands and looking straight ahead, but already Dixon's hand is rising up to cover his face, by the last photo he's fully concealed. There isn't a single shot of his entire face, but rather four shots of his face in varying degrees of cover.

"You can piece these together into a head shot?" I asked Fiona.

"Easy," she said. There was a more serious tone to her voice than I expected.

"Do you know him?"

"No," she said.

"He's not Special Forces," I said, though he had his game down, at least in terms of photos.

"No," she said, "he's not."

"I'd guess he wasn't even ROTC."

Fiona rearranged the photos on the table, put a hand over Cricket, then over Dixon's hair, then again across his midsection.

"Is there a reason he'd want to buy guns?" Fiona asked.

Before I could answer, my cell rang. It was Sam.

"Mikey," he said, his voice a barely audible whisper, "I'm in a bit of a . . . situation."

"Where are you?"

"Offices of Longstreet Security," he said. He gave me the address. It was near the airport, just a few miles away.

"Armed?"

"Them?"

"You."

"Not enough."

I checked my watch. "We'll be there in fifteen minutes."

"At the gate, if they ask, tell them you're with Chazz Finley," Sam said. "That's two Zs."

5

When you're Sam Axe, certain things come easy.

Women.

Free drinks.

Trouble.

Before he called me asking for help, Sam had spent the afternoon doing two things: One: getting Cricket O'Connor out of her house and into a safe temporary location, which, in this case, meant Veronica's place for a few hours, so he could . . . Two: learn as much as possible about Dixon Woods in hopes it would lead him to the man scamming Cricket.

He figured a trip down to Longstreet's offices would be as good a place as any to search for a man who, according to the government, didn't exist. Well, that's not entirely true: The FBI told Sam that Dixon existed from 1966 through 1984. Then existed in a number of different authorized government capacities. And then, upon discharge, some unauthorized capacities before latching on with Longstreet. But none of these roles had managed to require a valid passport, credit history or permanent address.

"Born in Portland, Oregon. Moved to Fort Lauderdale with his parents during high school. Entered the Army at age eighteen," one of Sam's sources told him, and then ran down the same information Sam already had. Strictly HR stuff. Sam's source was a guy named Kyle. Sam had never met Kyle in real life, thought that if he ever did meet him that he'd be about five foot one and ninety-seven pounds but would drive a Corvette. Sam had him pegged as a "nice-car-sorry-about-your-penis" type—a real compensator. That's why he'd always been such a great source for Sam over the years, even before the FBI made Sam my de facto watchdog, because Sam would regale Kyle with stories about hot missions and hot women and other hot lies, and Kyle would get all hopped up over them. He'd ask for minute details, which gave Sam the impression Kyle was using the stories for some other purpose in his afterwork life. Whatever. None of it was true, but if the kid liked it, who was Sam to pass judgment? Kyle was a computer jockey who liked to give Sam information in exchange for stories, and Sam was happy to comply. He hadn't even needed to actually tell a true story yet.

"You got a photo of him there, Philly?" Sam always called him Philly, because Kyle once told Sam he was originally from Philadelphia, so Sam figured the kid might like a nickname, and there was no way to make Kyle sound cool.

"His file has been wiped. All I can get you is his first driver's license photo."

That was a start. Better than anything else, Sam supposed, but not better than whatever Longstreet probably had. Sam tossed out one other thought. "There any Interpol reports on him?"

Sam could hear Kyle breathing hard on the other end of the line. Freaky kid. Getting off on this stuff probably, but whatever. Doing fine American service. "No, but there's a police report out of Jupiter, Florida, from two years ago. Misdemeanor disturbing the peace and assault. Charges were dropped. That's the only official line that's not sealed."

Jupiter was a hundred miles up the coast, but a very long way from Afghanistan. Odds were, if Dixon Woods got in trouble in Jupiter for something, it was the same guy Cricket O'Connor was married to, or was somehow connected to her. Guy like Dixon Woods, if he got caught doing something really severe, odds were fair he had enough government chits that he could call in a few favors. Sam knew something about that, for sure, which made him think of something else.

"What about a marriage license? To a Cricket O'Connor?"

There was nothing. Sam thanked Kyle, gave him a brief story about taking down a terrorist cell in Montreal—a little-known group of French-Canadian separatists, Sam told him—and when even Sam realized how absurd this was all getting, hung up and headed to the offices of Longstreet.

*   *   *

Longstreet was hardly an anomaly in Miami. Since Iran-Contra, the war on drugs, the first Gulf War, and then up through the second war on drugs and the war on terror, private paramilitary firms have popped up all over the world, essentially offering the same service everywhere: military expertise on an à la carte basis. But since the destabilization of Iraq and Afghanistan, groups like Longstreet have also become multimillion-dollar corporations willing to drop trained personnel into a hot zone for an appropriate fee. Diamond mines, opium fields, small cities and anywhere private security was needed. In Iraq, the United States actually subcontracted out firms to do the dirty work the military couldn't, by rule of international law.

Miami was home to a half dozen such firms. The reasoning was both natural and mundane: Florida works like a vortex for the international criminal trade, which is one of the chief employers of these firms, but it is also an easy access point into and out of the country to the unstable countries of the Caribbean, Africa and the Middle East, where most business is conducted. A flight from Miami to Dubai is just fifteen hours. An ambien away. Simple. Guyana, eight. Haiti, two.

And, in the realm of the mundane, there's no state income tax in Florida. Which means more money.

You want to find rich assholes with guns, find a state with no income tax, lax laws on personal firearms and easy access to one of the worst-secured ports in the country. That's Miami.

Plus, when people (or nations or warlords) want

to hire you, appearances matter. A Miami address? That says sun, splash, Don Johnson and superfit hired killers.

What Sam found, however, was a warehouse in an industrial park adjacent to the airport district. Surrounding the warehouse was a barbed-wire fence and a front entrance that looked particularly fortified.

Gaining entrance to a secure facility is about understanding how security consultants and the people who've hired them to design their alarm systems think. The first issue is that they are most concerned about keeping you out. So they make the front door look imposing.

Sam saw a keypad.

An infrared camera.

Titanium bars over blast-safe glass.

A sign that warned unwanted visitors that an armed response was already on the way.

Average crooks see these things, the first thing they are going to do is decide it's not worth the effort. Average sales person cold-calling cold-calls someone else.

The second issue is that like any other profession, security consultants are sloppy and human and prone to doing things in a half-assed way if they think appearances will be enough to stop inspection.

And that means, if you're lucky, all of the above will be proctored by a man with a clipboard sitting on his ass next to a plywood arm letting cars into and out of the facility, which is precisely what Sam found.

Fortunately, Sam hadn't bothered to change his clothes from the morning's activities, nor had he bothered to dip into a sports bar for a few hours. So he looked and smelled fresh, which worked to his advantage when he pulled up to the gate.

"Chazz Finley," he said to the guard. Sam stared straight ahead, trained his eyes on the cars in the parking lot, noted that it looked like a giant had crapped out the same ten brown Hummers right in a row.

The guard flipped through the papers on his clipboard. "Don't have you down here, sir," he said.

"Of course you don't," Sam said. He faced the guard now. Trying some of that Jedi shit. Confident. Stern. Not taking no for an answer. Official. After about twenty seconds of that, he said, "Are you going to wait here all day or do I have to drive through this gate?"

"Sir, I'm afraid you're not on the list." The guard put his hand on his gun, a real gun, not a toy like most security have, a little snub .22 or something. No, this guy was holding a .357. "Which means you're not getting in."

This was harder than Sam had anticipated. Usually, a guy working a gate is susceptible to double-talk, since at nine bucks an hour double-talk was too much trouble to fight with for most people. But this guy, he was some sort of monk with his mind-control abilities. He hadn't been trained. He'd been conditioned, and Sam actually appreciated that.

Nevertheless, Sam tried lobbing a grenade at him just to see the look on his face, hope for an inch of collateral, take a centimeter of recognition. A rat can get into a building if there's enough space under a wall for light to shine through. Sam figured Dixon Woods might be that light.

"I'm here about Dixon Woods." Sam spit out the name, figuring, *Hey, it's true. Let's see what happens?*

"Oh, yes," the guard said. He moved his hand from his gun like it was suddenly electric. "Very sorry." And like that, the plywood arm rose, and the guard went back to his post. Didn't even bother to get on the phone. Just went back to imagining it was five o'clock somewhere. A sentiment Sam could get behind, for sure.

Sam parked next to one of the Hummers, his Cadillac suddenly a dwarf. He never understood the desire people have to drive Hummers, particularly ex-military types. They always reminded him of the back pain he felt for the entire Cold War period he was involved in, hunched as he was in HumVees in places a helluva lot worse than an industrial park in Miami. You felt every bump in a HumVee. A Cadillac, well, that was like driving a Long Island iced tea. Power, grace earned through years of performance and, ultimately, comfort.

At the employee entrance to Longstreet was, predictably, another guy with a clipboard. At least this guy wasn't armed. He didn't even look of drinking age. Sam took a look at the guy's uniform and saw it was from Action Response Security.

Longstreet, one of the most powerful security firms in the world, with operatives in every conflict known and unknown, used rent-a-cops. But then, there was the natural question of just what they were keeping under cover. If there was anything with an outsized importance—ten thousand pounds of cocaine, maybe an actual poppy field grown hydroponically, things like that—they'd have their own guys at all points of entrance.

"Chazz Finley," Sam said to the man with the iron-on badge. His name tag said his name was Harvey. Harvey. Who named their kid Harvey anymore?

Harvey handed Sam a visitor's pass to clip to his shirt. "Keep this on you," he said. "It's my ass if you're walking around without it."

Sam winked, because that's what a guy like Chazz Finley would do, and Harvey opened the door for him. Before Sam walked in, but after seeing how empty and unsecure the corridors looked, he had a thought. "My associates will be joining me shortly," he told Harvey.

"Names?"

"Hard to say," Sam said and winked again, because when you're a guy like Harvey, a guy winking at you means you're part of a secret. And if you work at Longstreet, that's probably pretty cool, even if you just work the door. "And let Front-Door Freddie know about it, too. No screw-ups, Harvey."

"Understood, Mr. Finley," Harvey said. And then he gave Sam a salute. Christ, Sam thought. Poor sucker was going to lose his job.

When you think about the office space belonging to an elite security force, you'd probably imagine lots of blinking lights, massive computer screens on every wall detailing troop movements, satellite positions and the standing heart rate of every person currently in Longstreet's employ. You might think that the halls would be filled with people staring intently into files, shaking their heads, muttering about the military-industrial complex, maybe even holograms of Eisenhower and Patton that constantly spout motivational speeches if anyone with a body fat percentage under 25 percent walks by.

You'd be wrong.

Just like any other business where most of the sales are done outside the office, a successful multinational security firm is a pretty quiet place, the top guns more likely perched on a berm somewhere than in a cubicle; thus what's left behind is office staff. File clerks. Accountants. People in charge of ordering flak jackets and body armor and TEC-9s, but who were unlikely to need flak jackets, body armor and TEC-9s during the course of their own life.

Guys like Kyle versus guys like me and Sam.

All of which is good, because Sam wasn't looking for an armed conflict. He was just looking for records. Insight. A lead. A last known address. Anything to get us around Cricket's problem. And, it turned out, to see about my problem with Natalya as well.

In the lobby—which looked to be decorated with an eye toward reviving Communism as a design aesthetic and then combining it with some of the nicer floors of the Pentagon—Sam found an office map bolted to the wall. The bulk of the warehouse was taken up by a storage facility—Sam didn't need access to know what was in there, and why at least the front of the store was guarded by a man with a gun: assault rifles by the dozen, maybe a decommissioned Black Hawk or two, even more Hummers, a few rocket launchers, hell, maybe even a small nuclear sub if these guys were really pulling the bank in—while the administrative offices occupied a perimeter around the goods in a U.

Sam found what he was looking for. Across from the ladies' restroom and just adjacent to an emergency exit—a good thing to note—was the employee-relations office. A quick scan showed that the men's room was on the other side of the building, next to the office of the president.

You want to find the one woman working in a building likely filled with men, find the ladies' room and then count twenty paces, which, naturally, is precisely where the employee-relations office was.

Sam checked his reflection in his sunglasses—it wasn't going to get much better—and made his way down the hall.

The employee-relations office, like every other door Sam passed, was closed. The difference was that every other office was placard free, as if maybe all that was there was a door that opened into a brick wall. But right on the door was a sign that said EMPLOYEE RELATIONS and then, beneath it, a name: BRENDA HOLCOMB.

Sam gave the door a pound. It opened a few seconds later and revealed a woman in her midfifties. Her hair was straight and black and came down to her shoulders, though it looked like it had been cut using a rock. She wore a white buttoned-down shirt that she'd opened to the middle of her chest (where Sam saw a few red freckles and the outline of her sports bra) and a black skirt of, sadly, an appropriate length. Thick clunky sandals with heels probably two inches too tall. Painted toenails. Calves that showed about two dozen years of regular workouts. If pressed, Sam would guess she'd been an MP somewhere. She had that cop stance—one leg forward, one leg back, a hand on the hip reflexively, as if still looking for a gun, but instead holding a venti Starbucks cup.

More interesting, however, was that she had a lightning-bolt tattoo that started at her clavicle and shot up the right side of her neck, dying into her jaw line. It covered a jagged scar. That must have hurt, Sam thought.

"Who are you?" she said, all business.

"Finley," Sam said. There was always a Finley on the books.

"What do you need?"

"I'm here about that OSHA thing," Sam said. When Brenda just stared at him blankly in response—not mad, not confused, not suspicious, just not getting it—Sam added, "Iraq?"

"Oh, workers' comp," she said, her voice not unpleasant. Brenda opened the door and Sam got the full measure of her office. There were three file cabinets along the right wall, a garbage can overflowing with shredded paper, a desk that held two laptops and stacks of paperwork that didn't seem to have any order whatsoever. Two more venti Starbucks cups. On the left wall, there was a huge map of the world with white thumbtacks shoved into different regions. The Middle East was filled. Africa had scattered clumps. Afghanistan was covered corner to corner. The weird thing was the number of thumbtacks in Wyoming, Texas and Georgia. Who the hell needed paramilitary units in Wyoming? Maybe it was to keep the people in, stop them from infecting the rest of the country. There was a separate blown-up map just of Miami, with thumbtacks along different streets. "Have a seat," Brenda said, pointing to a white plastic chair covered in newspapers. "Just toss that crap onto the floor."

Sam did as he was told. It gave him time to look at the file cabinets. No one had file cabinets anymore. It was all digital. But Brenda, apart from her tattoo, seemed old school. That was a good thing.

"Where'd you get shot?" Brenda asked. She was yanking paper out of a drawer in her desk, compiling them into a stack.

Sam did a quick catalog of his body. He'd taken some bullets. "Back of the right thigh," Sam said. He doubted she'd ask him to strip down to see the scar.

"No," she said, "I meant where in the country?"

Sam took a look at the map. "See all the tacks? Right there in the middle."

Brenda laughed. She seemed like a nice lady. Apart

from that, Sam sensed that she actually wasn't a very nice lady. "We'll put down Sunni Triangle and let them figure it out," she said. She'd compiled about twenty pages of documents and was now going through them with a yellow highlighter and marking places where, presumably, he'd need to fill things out.

That wasn't going to happen.

"Nice ink," Sam said.

That did it.

"You think so?" Brenda said. She was staring at Sam now, trying to see if he was mocking her or if he meant it. Sam liked that. That little bit of unease on her part. Opened up some avenues of charm.

"Know so," he said. "How'd you get cut?"

"A knife, soldier," she said. Smart, like of course he was soldier. Now he was getting somewhere, could feel things changing in the room.

"That carotid is a bleeder," Sam said. "One time, in Caracas, I saw a guy milk out completely in under a minute. And that was with a Norelco Electric during a shaving accident." He had Brenda laughing again. "I like that you're not afraid of the scar. Highlight it. Own it. Pretty cool, you ask me. Gives you a real element of intrigue."

"Guys around here," she said, motioning around the building, "they call me Bolts now. Brenda Bolts. I guess I'm like a sister to them, mother to half of them, all of thirty, you know? But still, I'm not a robot."

No. No, you aren't, Sam thought. "How did it happen?" Sam used his quiet voice, let her know that he wasn't trying to get some sort of glee out of it, but that he was deeply, deeply concerned. Brenda (who he could only think of now as Bolts, thought, in fact, that it was a much more alluring name) told him a long and rather circumspect story about helping out on a mission in San Salvador two years ago—some on-the-ground work, paying off people, that sort of thing, when *shit got tight* and, well, next thing she knew, there was a knife to her throat and demands for her money or her life.

"I'm glad you gave your money," Sam said. He reached across the table and touched her lightly on the hand. Nothing sexual. Nothing overt. Just letting her know she had a friend who understood. He was surprised to find her hand shaking.

"Whew," she said, "it's like it's happening all over again. It does feel good to talk about it."

"They say talking about trauma splits it in half," Sam said. He didn't know where he heard that. Oprah? Maybe Dr. Phil.

"Isn't that true?" Brenda said and then she was uncomfortably silent.

The rat saw a space to squeeze through again. "You keep any beer here?" Sam said.

"It's a little early for that, don't you think?"

Sam didn't really consider it a question. More like a coconspirator making sure they were on the same job. Plus it was clear she wanted one, too, so he said, "I'm still on Iraq time," though not really sure he even knew what time it was in Iraq.

Brenda pushed back from her desk. "We could have one, right?"

"Of course," Sam said.

"Didn't you earn it, soldier?"

"Didn't *you*, soldier?" Sam felt his own skin crawling. But this Brenda, good old Bolts, seemed to fall for every line. You don't get any sympathy, even false sympathy probably felt pretty swell.

"It *is* lunchtime," she said, convincing herself. Sam liked that. Liked that in just a little over fifteen minutes he'd actually convinced Bolts to have a liquid lunch with him. "Why don't I run down to the kitchen, get us both a taste, maybe a bag of chips? There's no harm in that, right?"

"Right," Sam said. He pulled the stack of papers from in front of Bolts and a pen. "And I'll get started on these forms."

Brenda got up then, straightened her skirt and gave Sam a look that he usually associated with nature programs where a wildebeest finally figures out that the stream is filled with crocodiles but figures, *What the hell? Take a chance or two in life.* "Why haven't I seen you before?"

"Bad luck," Sam said and then, when that didn't seem like enough, added, "For both of us."

When Brenda left her office a few moments later, she still looked a bit puzzled but aroused. Sam figured he had maybe five minutes to get what he needed and get out before puzzled and aroused turned into suspicious and angry. He could still hear her heels clomping down the hall, like she was a

Clydesdale. Those calves. Man. He had to get to work before she got back and wanted to tussle. That might be a fight he'd lose.

His first thought was to jump onto the laptops, but he was for shit on a computer. Worst case, he'd take one of them and let Fiona work that. So he hit the file cabinets first, particularly since he could already see a drawer marked s–z and had a pretty good idea they'd contain at least something he could use.

He rifled through the files, finally finding Dixon Woods' toward the back. It was thick with work documents—close to an inch—so Sam took out his cell phone and just started clicking photos, figuring time spent examining the docs would be better done somewhere less . . . *armed*.

Problem was, the things he was taking pictures of were fairly meaningless. And old. Nothing newer than 2003, probably when they took everything and put it on the computers. He found requisitions for desert clothing. A stack of rental-car receipts from Japan. A purchase order for a GPS system and night-vision goggles.

Sam didn't even really know what he wanted to find, except that he knew a detailed list of Woods' actions over the course of the past fifteen years would be a bonus. A phone number, a mailing address, an idea of how whoever was sleeping with Cricket O'Connor and taking her money happened to come across Dixon would be even better, which got Sam to actually pause and think.

He sifted to the very back of the file and found

what he didn't know he was looking for: Dixon Woods' original application. Rather than take a photo, he just yanked it from the file and shoved it down his pants. Sam then went over to the map of Miami and clicked a few photos of that, too, particularly since he noticed several thumbtacks in South Beach and five on Fisher Island alone. A pretty high density.

It had taken him four minutes to do all of this, which Sam thought might be a personal record, but didn't feel like he had time to gloat. It was either get out or get trouble.

But that's the thing about Sam. Trouble finds him.

Just as he was about to walk out into the hallway, he heard Brenda Holcomb clomping back.

Plan A was that he could punch Brenda in the face and run out of the building. But he liked to avoid punching women in the face.

Plan B involved pistol-whipping Brenda and running out of the building. Again, he had a code about pistol-whipping women.

Plan C was a few drinks and maybe see where things went, though he really did like Veronica. And the Caddie. Why wreck a good thing?

Plan D was to just act like a dumb man.

He grabbed one of the Starbucks cups and dumped it across Brenda's desk and onto his pants. Sam popped his head out the door. "There you are," he said. Brenda had two bottles of Amstel in one hand—Sam could actually see the sweat coming off of them, like he was in some damned commercial and a bunch of sorority girls were about to pop out of a broom closet to get the party started—and a bag of tortilla chips in the other. Maybe, after all of this, after he retired, he'd look into a job at a place like Longstreet. Cold beers and chips in the company fridge had a certain appeal. "You think it would be okay if I used the ladies'? Seems I can't be trusted around a coffee cup."

"What kind of soldier are you?" Brenda said. He had to admit, this "soldier" stuff was pretty cute. He'd see about getting it worked into a fantasy or two down the line. Brenda got up close to Sam and examined his pants, took a gander inside her office, shook her head. Can't be the worse mess she's ever seen, Sam thought. "Better get some water on those before the coffee stains," she said. "Go ahead and use my bathroom, but don't tell anyone. They'll think I'm getting soft and think worse about you. Bad enough they've probably already seen you spilling the coffee on yourself."

Sam gave her one of his newfound winks and headed to the restroom, where, he realized, exactly what Brenda Holcomb had said, and realized, indeed, there was about to be a situation.

6

Most people don't want to get hit in the face. Who can blame them? Getting hit in the face hurts, but it's also expensive, especially if you don't have insurance. A severely broken nose? The kind you'd get if someone who knew how to hit you just right managed to hit you just right, thus collapsing your nasal cavity into your face but not actually killing you by shoving upward and into your brain? That's four to seven thousand dollars in plastic surgery just to get you looking human again. A blown-out orbital bone? That's another eight grand, plus there's always the chance you'll lose some sight. Broken jaw? That's a bad time: months drinking your meals out of a straw and then a bill for ten grand at the back end, along with maybe a few permanent metal plates in your face, just to keep things together.

If you're doing the hitting, you also don't want to hit someone in the face, unless you are certain you can find a soft spot, like the eyes or the bridge of the nose. Hit someone in the mouth, there's an excellent chance you'll end up with teeth lodged in your knuckles, which is hard to explain when you're at the hospital. Hit someone in the forehead, you're likely to pop the joint at the base of your pinkie, by far the weakest joint in your entire hand, or, if you're really unlucky and the person you're hitting is particularly hardheaded, crush all of your knuckles at one time.

You really want to incapacitate someone? You go for the throat. Or, barring that, you go for the ears. Mike Tyson was no dummy. Well, he was, but he knew how to spot vulnerability in an opponent and legalities never seemed to bother him.

I thought about this very issue as Fiona and I pulled up in the Charger at the front gate of Longstreet's offices. The security detail was standing in front of the gate with his back to us, talking on a walkie-talkie, so when he heard the car roll up, he turned and gave us an absent *halt* sign with his palm. Ahead of him I could see three beefy-looking fellows huddled around Sam's Caddie in the parking lot. All three were wearing workout gear—shorts, tank tops, New Balances—and I could see the sun gleaming off of their skin even from one hundred yards away.

Still, this didn't look good. If they were looking in the car, that meant they knew it didn't belong. And if they were outside in their workout gear, it was probably because someone had yanked them away from their free weights somewhere inside. I put the Charger in PARK and turned to Fiona. "Watch me," I said.

"Just run him over," Fiona said.

"If it looks like that's a viable option, go ahead." I jumped out of the car and started walking toward the guard. When Fiona slid behind the wheel, I said, " 'Scuse me. My lady and me, we can't find the airport. I see all these planes buzzing around, but for the life of me, can't find nothing."

The guard turned his head toward me. "What?"

I was about a yard away from him now. "The airport? Place with all the planes and people? I can't find it."

"Get back in your car," the guard said. "This is a secure facility." Not for much longer, I thought. He put his hand on the butt of his gun to prove his point nonetheless and probably because I was about a foot away from him now.

"No problem," I said. I raised my arms wide to show him I meant no harm and took a step backward.

When he turned his back to me again, he pulled out his radio and said, "I think he's under one of the . . . ," but before he finished, I clapped him simultaneously on both ears.

You do this hard enough, two things happen:

1. The person passes out.
2. The person vomits and *then* passes out, because you've turned their semicircular çanals into a centrifuge.

I hit him really hard.

The guard grunted and then vomit splashed out

of his mouth in a rushed torrent. At the same moment his knees went completely slack. Though I had to jump back to get away from the puke, I did manage to grab the guy by the waist to give him a soft landing. Bad day to be a security guard, but I figured there was no need for him to wake up with a broken neck. Still, I didn't want him causing too much more trouble, so I yanked his cuffs off of him—a nice pair of heavy-duty hinged cuffs, the ones you'd use if you wanted someone to be as uncomfortable as possible while being detained—hooked him to his guard shack and took his .357.

Fiona pulled the Charger up beside me and I slid into the passenger seat. I didn't really like the idea of Fiona driving my car. She didn't have a great respect for things like black-flecked paint on recently restored muscle cars from the 1970s.

"Sam just texted," she said. "He's hiding under one of the Hummers next to his Cadillac."

"What is he doing?" From our vantage point, we could see the Hummers but not Sam. I trusted that he was where he said he was.

"He apparently had to escape from the building but didn't want to leave his car behind," Fiona said. "He indicated there was an aggressively violent woman involved who he would prefer I not kill."

A woman who looked aggressively violent burst out the front door of the facility. She had a lightning bolt running the length of her neck. She also had a shotgun and two aggressively violent-looking men trailing behind her. There was a barbed-wire fence between them and us still, but not for long.

"I guess that would be her," I said. Sam popped out from under one of the Hummers and started running toward the gate. The men surrounding his Caddie hadn't noticed him yet, but I had a good feeling that would change momentarily when the woman with the shotgun rounded the bend, spotted us and spotted Sam running toward us. "Shit," I said. "Go."

"Where?" Fiona said.

"Get Sam," I said. "Go." Fiona beamed. "And try to avoid destroying my car."

Fiona punched the gas and the Charger shot through the gate, splintering the plywood arm across the bumper. Which hurt me. Not physically. But it hurt me.

The three men surrounding Sam's Cadillac whipped around at the sound of the Charger growling toward them, but seemed unsure what to do. This wasn't Fallujah, after all. And they didn't look armed.

And this was Miami. A 'seventy-four Charger pounding over the pavement could justifiably be driven by an octogenarian with a poor sense of direction.

Regardless, I rolled down my window and started shooting at the Hummers to give Sam some protection. Not surprisingly, my bullets pinged right off of them. Armor-plated. Nice. These guys were pros. Which also meant that at the first sound of gunfire, they did the right thing: They got down flat.

Behind us, the woman with the lightning bolt had no such compunction.

"You lying son of a bitch!" she shouted and then she fired a shot at Sam, who was now about ten yards from my car. She then screamed a few more things that were hard to accurately parse over the cocking and firing. Oddly, the woman didn't seem to want to hit Sam. She was firing way over everyone's heads.

And Sam wasn't shooting back.

Something weird was going on here.

Still. There were bullets.

And the guys by the Caddie had snapped alert and were now chasing after Sam.

"Cover me," I said to Fiona. I jumped out of the Charger and fired three times at the woman with the shotgun. And since she didn't seem to be actually shooting at Sam, I didn't actually shoot *at* her, either. Instead I destroyed the rack of cameras I saw lining Longstreet's fencing—cameras that were literally swiveling to capture all of the action.

At the same time, Fiona took care of the men chasing after Sam, except her method was to shoot at Sam's Cadillac, taking out all the windows, all the tires, and both mirrors. All in the course of about fifteen seconds.

She's a very good shot.

It was enough to get everyone on the ground, at least for a moment, and for Sam to dive into the backseat of my car.

When the woman started to rise, I put the gun on

her again. "I'm not trying to kill you," I said. I swung around and made sure the men behind the Charger saw me, and heard me, too. "But I will."

"That asshole stole something from my office," the woman said. That didn't seem to be the thing that was bothering her, though. She honestly looked heartbroken.

"I'm sorry about that," I said. "But it's no reason to come out here with a shotgun." I motioned for Fiona to get into the car. In the distance, I could hear sirens. Did these people actually call the police? Who calls the police anymore? What kind of paramilitary unit were they? "Whatever he took, he'll return it when we're done with it. As a token of trust, we're going to leave his car here." I pointed at the Cadillac, which wasn't exactly in driveable condition now anyway. "I'm going to get into my car. You'll have about three to five seconds where it will be possible for you to stand up and shoot me. That's a choice you can make. But understand that my friend behind the wheel will run you over and then she'll come back and kill everyone you know. That's just how she is."

This seemed to get everyone's attention.

"Do you know who we are?" the woman asked. "We will hunt you down through every corner of the universe."

I opted not to point out that the universe was unlikely to have actual corners, that it was likely more of a fluid concern. "I am well aware of who you are," I said. "You have a very comprehensive Web site." I started back toward the car. "But, honestly, your security? It's terrible. You might consider outsourcing." I slid into the Charger then, figuring, you know, they probably didn't have a witty rejoinder to bounce back off of me.

Fiona showed great restraint by only spinning the tires once before shooting back through the gate.

A 1974 Dodge Charger seats two comfortably, three if the person sitting in the rear seat happens to be an Olympic gymnast with tremendous flexibility or was unfortunately born without knees. If you want comfort, buy yourself a 1974 four-door Dodge Coronet. It has the same body type and plenty of police departments across the land found them to be excellent for ferrying passengers to prison.

If you intend to have a whining and complaining Sam Axe in your backseat, the Coronet also came with an optional eight-track tape stereo system that one could use to drown out Sam's voice. Three Dog Night or Mac Davis would be great choices. Mott the Hoople would work. Foghat. Anything to dampen the din.

"You did not need to do that to my car," Sam kept saying. At first, he just said it under his breath, I presume because he didn't want to sound like he was complaining, since we'd just saved his ass. And judging from his split upper lip and the way the tip of his nose was turned just slightly to the right, there was some validity to that presumption.

"What happened to your face?" I asked. We were already back on River Drive, crossing behind the airport and back toward my place. We could still hear the sirens in the distance.

"That woman with the shotgun," Sam said. Then: "Fiona, you didn't have to do that to my car."

"I know," Fiona said, "but I was happy to."

"No," Sam said, "I mean . . ."

"I know what you mean, Sam," Fiona said. "Your utmost gratitude is appreciated and duly noted."

"You didn't have to do that to my car," Sam said again. "Maybe you'd like to tell Veronica? Maybe just drop me off at a bar and you go back to Veronica's and explain that while she was kindly watching Cricket, you were blowing up my car."

Sam was shouting now.

He kept sputtering about loyalty and the durability of American cars and how he'd always wanted a car like that and now, now, where was he?

"Sam," I said. "About your face."

"I should have ducked," Sam said. He explained the particulars that led to his eventual holing up in the ladies' room.

"Bolts?" I said.

"It's got a certain allure, doesn't it?" Sam said. "I mean, even after she hit me with her phone, I still felt, in a different situation, maybe five, ten years down the line . . . who knows?"

"She has a real pâté de fois gras," Fiona said.

"You don't find a woman who can take a knife to the carotid every day," Sam said. There was wistfulness in his voice that I chalked up to the high likelihood he had a concussion. He explained then that after he called us, he tried to sneak out of the bathroom and out the emergency exit, but that Bolts met him in the hallway. He decided that the best option then would be to confess his blooming attraction for her, which she admitted to having as well, and just when he thought he'd able to woo her enough to get the hell out of her office alive . . .

. . . her phone rang. And then it was all over but the gunplay.

"All for a piece of paper," Sam said. He pulled Dixon Woods' crumpled job application out of his pants and handed it to me. "Fiona, do you realize that Cadillac is one of the few cars that have traditionally gone up in value?"

"I didn't know that," Fiona said. "I'll steal you an old one, then, if it would make you shut up."

I took a few moments and looked over the form. "Where did you say there was a police report on Dixon from last year?"

"Jupiter," Sam said.

"How far away is that? A hundred miles?"

"Something like that," Sam said.

"You think your guy at the FBI could get you an idea when Dixon was last in the country? Just a round number even."

"Probably," Sam said. He was still distracted by his Cadillac being blown apart and left for scrap at Longstreet. "Do you know what a hundred miles feels like in a Cadillac, Fiona? It feels like silk. Like you're driving on a highway made of silk."

"I can turn around," Fiona said. "Let Bolts have

her way with you. Shall I? Let her beat on your face some more. Maybe if she hit you just right, she could get your eyes to finally line up straight."

"I'll have you know that I didn't even attempt to hit her back," Sam said. "That's the kind of gentleman I am. But I did shoot up her office, which was probably a mistake. Did you know that you can get an armor-plated laptop now?"

I did. It made shooting them out of frustration a real option, particularly the Dells.

"Bolts would have gouged your eyes out and eaten them," Fiona said. I knew where this was all headed, but I was trying to pay attention to Dixon's application, and it's fun sometimes to remember the good old days when Sam and Fiona hated each other. "You do recall that event in New York, don't you, Sam? You recall how you folded like a hand puppet in the face of—"

"Okay, children," I said.

We drove in silence for about two minutes. And by silence, I mean that I could hear Sam breathing. He was also mumbling things. Fiona was drumming her fingers on the steering wheel.

A hundred miles.

I hadn't been that far out of the city of Miami since, well, since getting to Miami. "How fast do you think I'd heat up if I had to drive to Jupiter?"

"You wouldn't get out of Fort Lauderdale," Sam said.

About what I thought. "According to Dixon's job application, his mother lives in Jupiter. Linda Woods.

He lists that as his permanent address. I'm going to guess she found herself missing some part of her savings recently." I gave Sam back the application so he could see for himself. "You say you've got a driver's license picture coming in?"

"Yeah," Sam said. "But it's twenty years old. Probably looks like the keyboard player from the Cure in it."

"Cricket will be able to tell the difference," I said.

"You really think so, Mikey? She can hardly tell the time right now."

"She'll know," I said. "You sleep with someone a few times, you know them well enough to spot a baby picture."

"That true, Fiona?" Sam asked. An olive branch. A bit of pleasant banter.

"I wouldn't know," she said. "Michael never was much for showing off mementos from his childhood," Fiona said. Everyone was chippy. "Just all the terrible, terrible mental scars. Isn't that right, Michael?"

"Anyway," I said, because what I didn't need was Fiona's wrath acknowledged again. Let Sam deal with that. "I'm going to guess Linda Woods' son wasn't real happy about her losing whatever she lost. We get back to my place, call your guy. Get a copy of that police report. Whoever made the complaint, that's our Dixon."

"Nice bit of revenge, taking his name," Fiona said. "Maybe I'll start going by Natalya Choplyn."

"That's funny," I said.

"Isn't it?" Fiona said.

No, not really, I thought. Instead, I said: "Do you really think that guy in the photo tried to buy guns from you?"

"Yes," she said.

"When was that?"

"Six months ago. Maybe less."

"I don't recall you selling any guns six months ago."

"That's because I didn't tell you."

"Keeping secrets is wrong," Sam said.

"So is back hair," Fiona said. "We pick our battles, don't we?"

"How many did he buy?" I asked, ignoring them both. The sooner we were out of this car and back in a place where I was fairly certain they wouldn't start hitting each other and somehow place me in peril as a result, the better. Until such time, I was Switzerland.

"None," she said. "We were to meet in the lobby of the Mandarin Oriental to discuss prices. But when I got there and saw him, I had a sense that perhaps he was not the kind of person to keep their mouth closed about illegal arms."

"Why was that?" I asked.

"He was wearing a shirt that said *Co-Ed Naked Volleyball* on it," Fiona said

"Classy," I said.

"And the hotel was filled with real estate agents attending a conference. I watched him for a time and he seemed to know many of them, or at least he said hello to them all. My impression was that he'd look lovely in one of those yellow coats, or with his head on top of a sticky calendar. The amount of perfume and large hair in that hotel was enough to turn me off."

"How did he contact you initially?" I asked.

"Through channels," she said.

"Fi."

"We all have secrets, Michael," Fiona said, "that are better left unknown to certain third parties who deem secret keeping wrong."

"Wrong is blowing up someone's car," Sam muttered.

"Fi."

"Fine, Michael," she said, and then went on to explain that she received a call from someone named Etienne, who'd received a call from Mario, who'd received a call from Gwyneth, who'd met a man named Holton, who knew a person who was looking for three AK-47s, of which Fiona was known to have easy access to.

Which is the definition of *channels*. None of those people were likely to know anything, less likely to, even if they did know anything, say a damn word.

"How long will it take you to put together that online profile?" I asked.

"A few minutes. All I'll really need is a photo and some interesting hobbies to punch it up. Maybe something about loving sex with overweight men and giving money away by the bushel."

"How long to get that head shot together of Dixon, or whoever he is?"

"No time at all," she said.

"Good," I said. "We get that picture. We get that license photo. We get the name off the police report, and we're in business." Just when I was about to suggest that Fiona and Sam could get over their differences concerning her shooting up his Caddie by riding to Jupiter together tomorrow to talk to Linda Woods, my cell phone rang.

It was my mother. I decided to let it go to voice mail, but the problem was that having it go to voice mail meant my mother would leave a thirty-minute-long message that would be more painful to listen to than the actual five-minute conversation I could reasonably have with her prior to *losing service*. So, even after deciding I'd let it go to voice mail, I answered it.

"I'm in a meeting, Ma," I said.

"Who are you meeting with?"

"Very important world figures. We're discussing how often they call their mothers. What do you need?"

"Some people came by the house looking for you," she said.

"When?"

"About two hours ago."

"What kind of people?"

"They talked like Communists."

"Ma, you need to be a bit more specific."

"They dropped off a package for you. They said you'd know what it was about."

"Is it ticking?"

"Michael, I'm not stupid."

That was true. But she was frustrating. "Does it smell like cordite?"

"It smells like a manila envelope, Michael."

"They leave any instructions?" These days, it was hard to tell who might drop by, good guys or bad guys.

"Yes," she said. "They said that they were bringing something to Nate's house, too, but that they'd wait to hear from you first."

"Nate?"

"They seemed to know him," she said. "Are you two working together again? It's always so nice when you include him. You know, he told me last week that he really feels close to you now. Isn't that nice?"

Fiona pulled up in front of my place. There was already a line of people waiting to get into the club and it wasn't even dark out yet.

"Where is the package now, Ma?"

"I put it in the bathtub . . . just like you taught me last time."

My mother, full of surprises. "I'll be there," I said. "Don't touch it."

If you ever happen to become a spy and then happen to get burned and are forced to live in one town under threat of death, try not to make it the same one your mother lives in. In the event that is unavoidable, at some point ask your mother to unlist her phone number and cancel, finally, the subscription to *Highlights* that still comes to her home in your name. See about getting her to move permanently into an assisted-living facility that doesn't allow smoking or outside phone calls. See about getting your brother to leave town, too, particularly if he happens to be named Nate. See about asking the people who are burning you if, respectfully, they could drop you in Walla Walla, Washington.

"I'll make dinner," Mom said. "Why don't you ask Fiona if she'd like to come?"

"I don't know where she is," I said.

"I'll call her," Mom said and hung up.

I closed my phone and got out of the car. Stood on the sidewalk. Stared up at the sun. Surveyed the people lined up under my window. I could hear rap music coming from inside the club, a song about never being caught riding dirty. I tried to think pleasant thoughts.

Sam unwound himself from the backseat and stood beside me on the sidewalk. Fiona? She was still sitting in the front seat of the Charger. Seems she'd received a call.

"That was my mother," I said to no one in particular.

"Nothing says you have to answer," Sam said. "A little self-control, Mikey, it will save you heartache."

"She was visited by Communists today," I said.

"They're like cockroaches. You see one, there's another hundred meeting somewhere."

"I don't think that's true anymore," I said.

"The Red Menace would surprise you, Mikey."

"This Natalya thing," I said. "I've gotta get around that, it seems."

"I saw something interesting today," Sam said. He flipped open his phone and scrolled through the photos until he found the one of Longstreet's map of operatives. South Beach looked like a conflict zone.

"Well," I said, "that is interesting." Particularly, I noted, the cluster surrounding the Hotel Oro. I thought about the meat guarding Natalya. I thought about the morons parking cars. I thought about maybe seeing just how much they'd like seeing their pictures in *Palm Life*.

Fiona popped out of my car then. She was still talking on the phone. "Pot roast it is," she said. "I'll bring some potatoes."

7

If you're at home and don't have access to the bomb squad, the best way to open an envelope that you think might contain an explosive charge is to not open it at all. Throw it in a tub filled with water or stick it in your toilet. Within two or three minutes, you'll be able to see precisely what is inside of the envelope.

If you see wires, a stick of TNT, hundreds of ball bearings, nails, a blasting cap, the odds are someone wants to kill you.

Don't open your letter.

If on the off chance the person you think wants to kill you was smart enough to send you a bomb in a waterproof, plastic-lined cardboard mailer, and you still have a latent desire to know for sure if someone wants you dead or disfigured, all you need is a piece of wire and some string, strong nerves, and a few yards of space between you and the envelope.

People who build letter bombs are big on bangs, particularly if they happen to be in the vicinity of the person opening the letter. The sound of the explosion, the flying limbs, the burned corpses, that's their thing. That means they leave the creativity to the bomb itself. The trigger is an afterthought. 80 percent of letter bombs are activated by opening the top flap of the envelope. 15 percent go off when the materials are removed. 5 percent never go off at all, because if you send someone a letter bomb, you're crazy and crazy people sometimes forget important steps in the building of bombs.

Ex-KGB? Not so much. So, as I stood in my mother's bathroom and stared at a wet plastic-lined cardboard mailer that revealed only that the persons who dropped off this package for me knew the same things I did, Fiona stripped apart a length of coaxial cable until she had a span of sharp wire about a foot long. She carefully inserted the cable through the bottom of the envelope and then threaded it back out and looped it around a piece of yarn that my mother swore she couldn't part with, since she intended to use it to knit me a winter scarf, but which I told her I'd replace with a whole ball of yarn if I accidently blew up her bathroom.

I then placed a frying pan on one end of the envelope, fastening it in place on the bathroom floor.

Fiona and I backed slowly out of the bathroom, keeping the yarn slack as we walked down the hall, back toward the kitchen, where the smell of pot roast still hung in the air an hour after we'd eaten.

My mom walked up with a cigarette in her mouth, lighter at the ready. "Be careful, Michael. I just redid that bathroom," she said.

"That was in 1996," I said. "And if you like the way it looks, you'll maybe keep the open flame away."

"I've been smoking all day and nothing happened," she said. "I don't know when you decided you had all the answers, anyway."

"Ma," I said, "you might have noticed that I'm a little involved with something here. Maybe keep back? In case it blows?"

"Don't use that soothing voice on me," she said. "Your father used that voice. It's unbecoming. I don't know how you stand him, Fiona."

"I can't," Fiona said. This got a chuckle from Mom. It was like I was trapped in a surrealist painting, surrounded by melting clocks and such—that's about how much sense it all made.

"Ma," I said. "Please. Go outside. If you see flames leaping from the windows, call nine-one-one."

For approximately the third time in her life, my mother actually did what I asked her to do.

"You could be nicer to her, Michael," Fiona said. "She made you a lovely dinner."

"If nothing blows up," I said, "I pledge I will spend the rest of my life trying to be a better person. Could we get this done?"

Once we were a reasonable amount of space away, Fiona gathered up the yarn until it was taut. She yanked the yarn and split the envelope in half. Nothing went bang. We waited another thirty seconds, in case there was a secondary trigger set to a timer, and when nothing happened we went back into the bathroom. I bent down and picked the package up and pulled the contents—wrapped a second time in plastic, most likely because they knew I'd try to submerge the package in water first—out through the bottom. I then shook the package out over the toilet, just in case there happened to be a dose of anthrax for my troubles.

I opened the package up. There were several glossy, professional-quality photos and a stack of black-and-white photos as well. Today, if you can't get a decent photo of someone from surveillance, you either have early onset Parkinson's, which causes you to shake uncontrollably, or you like kicking it old school with a Polaroid, just to show technology isn't needed if you're savvy, which makes you a useless dinosaur who should be burned versus those who do their job, do it well and lose everything anyway.

We went into the dining room and spread everything out on the table. Out the window, I could see my mother standing on the sidewalk smoking. It was always a strange experience being back in my childhood home as an adult, doing things completely unrelated to the person I was when I lived here as a child. If I closed my eyes and just relied on my sense of smell and the sounds whirring in the background—the smell of cooked meat, old cigarette smoke, damp coffee grounds, the hiss of the refrigerator, the cycling of the dishwasher, the slow turn of the overhead fan—I could easily imagine myself eight, nine, ten years old.

But here I was, fixed on a photo of me and my mother not eating lunch at the Oro.

"A nice establishing shot," I said.

"Two hundred years of espionage and they can't think of anything better?" Fiona said.

She spoke too soon. The next photo was of me talking to a passel of Jamaican drug runners on a dock in the Glades. It was from the air, but you could still see me. Could still see the drug runners. Could make out their boat. Another one with heroin smugglers, ex–Special Forces guys who nearly killed Sam. Again, from high above. There were more just like this. Over a dozen. All from the air.

"How long have they been tracking you?" Fiona said.

"Long enough."

"Drones?" Fiona asked.

"Maybe. Looks more like satellite. See the resolution? That's five, maybe six inches."

"Whose?"

"Could be Russian," I said. There was a photo of me with Philip Cowan, the man I thought had pulled my original ticket, moments before he was shot. "Could be ours. Could be the Chinese, for all I know." There was a photo of me in Little Haiti, meeting with a drug dealer. Another with a member of a notorious Colombian crime syndicate. "Jesus. They've got me with every known drug dealer in Miami. The close-ups, those could be FBI, but this

overhead work? With this clarity? It's not like someone was flying a kite with a camera on it. Jesus."

Fiona was silent. Never a good sign. I continued
looking through the pictures. There were shots of
Nate at the dog track. Nate at the jai alai stadium.
Shots of Nate unloading what looked to be an entire
rack of men's suits from the back of a semi. Shots of
Nate doing just about everything I imagined Nate
did in his free time when he wasn't helping old ladies do their taxes and going door to door selling
encyclopedias for the blind.

Nate.

My little brother.

The bane of my existence at his worse.

My brother, finally, finally, when at his best. It's
been the process of teaching him that being at his
best is the choice to make. We have the same parents,
so I understand how difficult that decision must be.

"What does this all mean?" Fiona asked, though I
suspected she already knew.

"That I'm not just burned," I said. "If they want
to build a case that I'm running drugs, or at least
facilitating such, as they like to say, there's a good
amount of evidence. Enough that the Russians are
using it to pressure Natalya, maybe make her kill
me, or make it impossible for her not to kill me.
If I'm Natalya and I get this intel, you know what
I think?"

"That you lied to her yesterday," Fiona said. "That
you've got plenty of reasons to shuffle anything off
on her if it means saving your own ass."

"Exactly," I said.

"Now can I kill her?"

"No."

"She'd never see it coming," Fiona said, but already we both knew that wasn't true. If someone had satellite images of me, there was an above-average chance that she could get a muffled recording of this very conversation if someone, somewhere, thought it pertinent for her to have.

What I didn't understand yet was what any of this had to do with Nate, why they'd even bother mentioning him after I got this message.

I went back and looked at the photos of Nate. The differences between Nate and me are easily boiled down: He has always been obvious. Took chances when he didn't need to. Played the tough guy when he really wasn't one and got beat down for his troubles. And now? Now that I was home? Was it my job to keep him safe? To keep him from his own screw-ups? I couldn't be blamed if he acted according to his nature, which was to act before thinking.

Which, I supposed, they knew as well. Whoever they were. The odds were good that Nate would just open his mail, provided the return address wasn't from a collection agency, and that a few seconds later he'd be missing his hands, or his face, or both.

At the bottom of the stack of photos was a Post-it with a phone number on it.

An 800 number.

"That's nice," Fiona said.

I punched the numbers into my phone. "Yes," I

said. "Thoughtful. I keep my brother alive, but they pay for the phone call."

The phone rang three times before it was answered. "Hotel Oro, how may I direct your call?" the operator asked.

"I'd like to speak to the Russian Mafia," I said.

"Pardon me?"

"KGB, please," I said. "Or ex-KGB. Whoever is available."

"I'm sorry, sir, but—"

"Ms. Copeland, please," I said. "If you're unsure who that is, just ask if anyone there has a scar on the back of their neck from a knife fight. It didn't keloid, but you should be able to see it if no one cops."

"One moment please, Mr. Westen," the operator said, because it's impossible to get good help anywhere these days, and then Muzak filled my ear.

"I've been put on hold," I said to Fiona.

"A true lack of disrespect," Fiona said.

My mother walked back inside, saw us sitting at the table and sat down next to Fiona. "Were you just going to let me stand outside all night?"

She shook out another cigarette and lit it off the end of the one in her mouth.

"Yes," I said.

She started fingering through the photos, picked up one of Nate and stared at it. "What's he doing with all of those suits?"

"Ma, I'm on the phone and this doesn't involve you," I said. I tried to gather up the photos, but my mother kept snatching them from me.

"What does Nate need a suit for?"

"He doesn't," I said. As soon as I'd grab a picture, my mother would snap it from me. "It's been Photoshopped. It never happened."

"Who are these men with the boat? And why do you look so grainy?"

"Fiona, a little help here?"

Fiona put her arm over my mother's shoulder. "Those men in the boat were Jamaican gangsters," she said.

"Oh," my mother said. It wasn't terribly new information to her, but I'd prefer keeping my business life and my personal life and my *mother* life as separate as possible, for days just like these. You get burned, you make do with certain new realities, like your mother knowing your business. Intimately.

"The photos are grainy because they were taken from outer space," Fiona said.

"By who?"

"Most likely aliens," Fiona said.

Sometimes, Fiona isn't much of a help.

Just when I was about to start explaining what I could—and what was needed—the Muzak stopped. I got up from the table and made my way outside, figuring whatever happened in this conversation, the less Mom knew, the less I'd need to explain later.

"Did you get my package?" Natalya asked.

"You didn't need to involve my mother and brother in this."

"I didn't," she said. "You're right."

"You've made it personal, Natalya."

"I wanted you to understand that if you sic your little pit bull on me, it wouldn't stop," she said. "You've been a busy boy, Michael. I almost believed you yesterday. Almost bought into your *Poor me, I've lost my job* talk. The pictures tell a compelling story, Michael."

"That's what it is: a story."

"I am expected to believe that you were meeting with those people out of goodwill? This might surprise you, Michael, but I know you. I know what you're capable of. I know what you've done. I know what you do. Goodwill isn't who you are."

"I've had to make a living these last few months," I said. "Not everyone can park themselves in a hotel. You kill enough, maybe you start to think differently of people, the ones who need something. Anyway, I don't require your approval. Or anyone's."

"My sources paint a different picture. You're in the drug trade now. That's fine with me, Michael. It doesn't suit your temperament, but I suppose you need to find your thrills where you can. It can't always be about espionage and sex with the wrong people."

I was standing beside the garage, where I'd spent half of my childhood working with my dad on one failed project after another, including the Charger, listening to a woman I'd once slept with, who'd tried to kill me, who I should have killed the several times I had the chance, telling me who I was, what I was about, telling me that what I was . . . wasn't.

"Natalya," I said, "I've lost patience."

"I can see that," she said.

"I'm sure you can." It was dark out, but the sky was clear. Since I grew up in your average poorly lit neighborhood, and since no one had bothered to complain to the city about how, after dusk, the streets fell into perfect blackness, interrupted only by the flickering of the same flickering streetlights that have flickered for nearly thirty years, I was able to see a full array of stars. I tried to spot any that seemed to be moving. Or blinking. Or snapping photos. "Your sources have quite an array of satellites," I said.

"Now you can see why I believe him."

"So he's a he?"

"Michael," she said, "do you think semantics are going to solve our problem?"

"This isn't *our* problem. I know what I have and haven't done. I've done bad things—that's true—but I didn't roll on you to cover my own ass. I don't even have an ass anymore. You're free to believe what you want to believe, but now you're going to have to pay the consequences, too."

"The consequences? Do you want to know the tally of a person's life, Michael? What your lies are worth? What our lives are finally worth to the nations we've worked for? Three million dollars. That's what the cut is. That's what I owe and therefore that is what you owe if you wish to live through this."

"Do not threaten me," I said.

"You should spend more time with your family," Natalya said. "Have you seen your brother lately?"

"Natalya," I said, "Nate is not part of this. My mother is not part of this. You and me, that's all this is."

"Is that true?"

Of course it wasn't. "Of course it is."

"You should watch the news, then," she said. Her accent, so perfect when I saw her yesterday, so British, was beginning to falter. Her inflection had changed. I didn't know if it was her atavistic self coming through her anger, or she was just tired of pretending. Either way, she was the woman I remembered, finally. "Your little assault on Longstreet made the five o'clock. I hope you've learned what you needed. Because next time? Next time they will shoot to kill."

"I'm sorry. I don't get TASS on my cable plan," I said, because suddenly, things were becoming clear to me. My problems, two of them, but not all of them, had that locus point I'd been searching for, that connective tissue. "And just so you know, Natalya, your body? Everything in it? All the skin, all the elements, all the fluids? The final tally is about five bucks. Use it wisely."

Natalya started to say something else, but I was already hanging up.

The time for talking to Natalya?

Done.

I went inside, had another piece of pot roast, told Fiona I wanted her to stay the night with my mother. Called Nate, told him not to open any of his mail and that if anyone came to his door, he should shoot them first, figure out what they wanted second, and if there was any problem to call me and I'd be there, but that I didn't have time to explain everything to him just yet, only that tomorrow, I'd need him. Called Sam, told him to get Cricket and bring her to my mother's, because we needed to keep things close at hand. Told him we needed to get Cricket's house ready for an operation tomorrow. Called an associate named Barry, who handles things like large sums of laundered money, and told him to meet me for breakfast.

Then I called the offices of Longstreet Security and left a message on Brenda Holcomb's voice mail, told her that my name was Hank Fitch and I was the guy who could have killed her and didn't, but would like to return what had been taken from her office, provided that the police weren't still snooping around and that she'd put her shotgun away. "And do me favor," I said into her voice mail, because I was feeling lucky, and because I was feeling cocky, and because I knew I was right, and that eventually I'd need someone like Dixon Woods, whoever he was, to be pissed off and in Miami. "Let Dixon Woods know that I've taken care of that problem his mother had up in Jupiter."

I didn't know if I knew what I was talking about, exactly, but I figured if Brenda Holcomb called me back the next day, I'd be on the right path.

Whatever *that* was.

8

The difference between being a spy and being a criminal is largely one of sanctioning. But when you've lost your sanction, it's important to know a few people who don't live on the right side of the law and don't care that you, for most of your life, did. Trust is the most important aspect of any relationship, but when you have two people with their particular agendas, agendas that might work at divergent angles, it's also important to have a strong sense of honor.

You like someone, you don't fuck them. At least not in business. You don't always find affinity with the people you work with, so the people you do, well, you foster it. In the end, if there is one, you'll have someone watching your back even if they don't exactly agree with who you are, or what you've done.

Which is why I didn't mind too much when Barry said he'd like to meet me at the Cereal Bowl in Coral

Gables for breakfast. It's a restaurant that serves cereal. They also have supersweet parfaits and coffee, but mostly, it's just cereal. Lucky Charms. Cookie Crisp. Trix. And since it's across the street from The U, every college student not on the meal plan is there drying out from the night previous.

When I got to the restaurant, Barry already had two empty bowls in front of him and was looking back over the menu again with a rather studious expression.

"What's your poison?" I asked, sitting down.

"Been mixing it up," Barry said. "First bowl was Kix. Second bowl was something from the Count Chocula family. I'm thinking I might try some of this Kashi stuff."

"I'm a Peanut Butter Cap'n Crunch man myself," I said.

"You're out of luck," Barry said. "They don't carry the Peanut Butter Cap'n here. Some union thing."

"It's okay," I said. "I don't actually eat cereal."

Barry pulled down his sunglasses and regarded me. Barry was the kind of guy who wore sunglasses inside. Barry was also the kind of guy who did creative things with his beard, so that it cut across his face in sharp angles. Barry was also the kind of guy who knew things about things you didn't know about, namely of the criminal variety. If Barry had a business card, it would say *money launderer* on it, but he had a lot of special skills. He was a confidence man in the truest sense: He kept things confidential. "You work out?" Barry said.

"A little," I said.

"I gotta start doing that, get off the cereal, get on the treadmill. What do you think of that Chuck Norris exercise device?"

"Bow-flex?"

"Yeah."

"Couldn't hurt," I said

"Three in the morning, that infomercial comes on?" Barry said. "It takes every fiber of my being not to get on the phone and order one. Chuck Norris is very persuasive."

"Nothing good happens after two a.m.," I said.

"True, true," Barry said. A waiter came up then. Barry ordered something called the Dirt Bowl. I just asked for a glass of juice. "What do you normally eat for breakfast?"

"Al-Quaeda," I said. "Or yogurt."

"Good to know," Barry said.

I could talk diet all day with Barry, but figured I'd get down to it. "If you had a couple million in cash, where would you put it right now?"

"Under the mattress," Barry said. "This recession is killing me."

"Say you weren't that smart."

"Diamonds and art are out," he said. "All that blood-diamond business is making people turn their backs on the bling. And with art, every two weeks someone is getting held up at gunpoint for a Gauguin. Getting shot in the face for water and ink on paper, that's not my idea of wise investing. Gold is a nonstarter. Rare coins have been ruined by eBay.

Same with vintage stamps. If you can get your hands on laser-guided missile technology, we could do business. My opinion? Get yourself someone legit as a front and you buy yourself a gas station."

The waiter came back then and dropped off Barry's order, which was completely made up of chocolate cereals, and my orange juice.

"This isn't for me," I said. "You ever hear of a guy named Dixon Woods?"

"Yeah," Barry said. He was trying to figure which milk to pour on his bowl. I pushed the skim milk in his direction, not that it would make a damn bit of difference. "Good example. He was around a lot last year. He fronted cash on a couple retail projects, probably made a killing. Haven't heard his name since."

"You ever see him?"

Barry shook his head no. "Everyone said he lived in a compound out there on the Fish. That he was some bad ass. People threw his name around like a threat. Figured you probably knew him."

"Where'd his money come from?"

"Big-game drugs. What I heard? He had his own opium field in Afghanistan."

"Where'd you hear that?"

"Around," Barry said.

"He move any locally?"

"Naw," Barry said. "He just chilled on the Fish. You ever see *Apocalypse Now*? I heard he lived like Brando did in that."

"People call Fisher Island *the Fish*?"

"No," Barry said. "But I do. Ten years ago, no one called diamonds bling." I took a sip of my orange juice while Barry shoveled down some of his cereal. The milk had already turned brown from the chocolate. It literally was like watching someone eating dirt. "You want a taste?" Barry asked.

"I'll pass."

"Anyway, point is, Woods was putting straight cash into projects that weren't likely to get looked at too closely. You know the Fish is privately owned, for instance."

"I didn't," I said.

"You got real estate money you don't want anyone to look at," he said, "you invest in three places: Indian land, private islands or the tourist trade. Bars. Strip clubs. T-shirt shops. I mean, you got a plane, a couple tough guys to fire guns at people, make your way to Africa or Haiti, but you gotta stay Stateside, that's your haven. Plus, a place like the Fish, it's all billionaires out there. You don't get a billion dollars by working straight. So if you've got two, three million to put down in real land to start up an espresso place, you think Bill Gates and Oprah are going to ask questions?"

"They live out there?"

"Metaphorically speaking," Barry said.

I pulled out the photo Fiona cobbled together using the shots from *Palm Life*. Sam had yet to get the paperwork from his contact at the FBI, so this was all I had. "You know this guy?"

"Don't know if I do," Barry said.

"Would you tell me?"

"Probably not." Barry swallowed up the last bits of his cereal. The bowl was still filled with chocolate milk. "What's the protocol here? Think I can tip it and drink it?"

"What would Chuck Norris do?" I said. That was enough for Barry. He picked up the bowl and slurped its contents down. The waiter came by and asked us if we'd like anything else. "Another bowl of dirt for my friend," I said.

"Easy on the Cocoa Krispies," Barry told the waiter.

"Say you did know this guy," I said.

"Say I did."

"Any idea where I might be able to find him?"

"Wherever there are rich old ladies," Barry said.

"Do you have a name?"

"Ronnie. Bobby. Ricky. Lonnie. Like that." There was a real look of disgust on Barry's face and palpable spite in his voice.

"Did he screw you on something?"

Barry took off his sunglasses, dabbed his napkin into a glass of water and took a few moments to wash off the lenses. The waiter came by and dropped off another bowl of cereal. "Strictly my opinion? You steal from old ladies, I don't care if they are rich, you bring disgrace on the whole criminal profession."

Made sense and I told Barry that. My cell phone rang. It was Sam. I excused myself and stepped outside. A line had formed to get into the Cereal Bowl. I tried to see if I recognized anyone from the line that usually gathered outside my place. Everyone looked familiar. In the future, people would wait in line to wait in line.

"What do you have, Sam?"

"A name," Sam said. "Eddie Champagne."

"That has to be an alias," I said.

"No," Sam said. "It checks. He filed the report on Woods two years ago after Woods kicked down his apartment door and smacked him around a little bit, but then dropped the charges."

"There statements?"

"Yeah. Woods says Champagne ripped his mother off, but Woods' mother says it's not true. They were in love. She gave him the money. Regardless, someone got Champagne to pull it back off the books."

"Does Champagne have a sheet?"

"Fraud. Bad checks. Theft. A gun charge."

"There you go. What else?"

"Cricket's call came in," Sam said. "The bad guys are coming tonight."

"Perfect," I said. "What about the picture of Dixon? Cricket recognize him?"

"No. I got my guy to pull Champagne's mug. No surprises there. It's her husband. Or not her husband."

"How'd she take that?"

"Your mom just kept pouring her drinks," Sam said.

"That's always been one of her best solutions. Something's wrong, throw a little alcohol on it. Apart from that, how are they getting along?"

"Like old friends."

"Really?"

"No," Sam said.

"No," I said. "I didn't figure that would be much of a match. Try to keep everyone placated. If you have to, lock my mother in the garage. Just throw in a carton of cigarettes and tune the TV to E! and crank up the sound. She'll be perfectly content."

"There's something else," Sam said. "I got a call this morning from D.C."

"Yeah."

"Whoever Natalya's source is has people listening," he said. "And talking."

"And?"

"That's all they said."

"Any line on who this is?"

"Someone who doesn't want you coming off the blacklist," Sam said.

"Did you tell them it's crap? I mean, Sam, you were there for these things."

"Michael, if I tell them I was there, I'm just as culpable if people really start listening. It's my pension. It's my career. All of it."

"You think I don't know that?" I said.

"I know you do," Sam said.

"Listen," I said. "I think we can take care of all of our problems. Meet me at Cricket's. Bring Fiona, too."

I hung up with Sam and went back inside. Barry was working on his new bowl. It was frankly starting to bother me in a real visceral way, so I didn't sit back down. "Let me ask you something," I said. "If I wanted to get a legit loan on a property, but get someone to appraise it higher than it was worth, set up dummy mortgage accounts, fake a credit history, how quickly could you set something up without drawing any attention to yourself?"

"If you're good, that's not a concern."

"Consider it implied," I said.

"For you?"

"For anyone."

"Trusted business associates, I could get it done in one business day. Two at the most. Normal friendly percentages, of course. How quickly the bank would fund the loan would be up to the bank."

"Forget the actual loan. Just the approval."

"Same deal. But you need the money, I could probably route that in under a week."

"What about someone who bought you a delicious breakfast and who hates to see the criminal profession disgraced?"

Barry considered this. "Three hours on the dummy stuff and approval. Twenty-four on the loan. Maybe less."

"I'll be in touch," I said.

"I know you will," Barry said. "As always, remember who helped you."

"Impossible to forget," I said.

Used to be, I helped myself. Used to be, I only called in support when I was really cornered, when there were tanks on the horizon and SCUDs in the air. Now here I was, in a cereal restaurant, talking to a guy with funny facial hair.

What was it they used to say? A new world order.

* * *

Twenty minutes later, while I stood in the chemical supplies aisle at Lowe's, my cell phone rang again. Perfect timing.

"Hank Fitch," I said.

"Who the fuck are you?" the voice on the other line said. I was expecting a woman. I was expecting Bolts, specifically, but this was a man.

"Hank Fitch," I said again. No reason to give my entire résumé.

It was a good ten seconds before the man on the other end of the line responded. "Do you know who the fuck this is?"

"Fascinating question," I said. I was looking for a cleaning product that had the appropriate amount of sodium bisulfate in it for a little project I was going to take on later that afternoon.

Another ten seconds went by. "You some sort of joker?"

I hadn't had a conversation like this since high school. I had a pretty good feeling I knew who I was talking to, so I hung up. Judging by the ten-second delay, my guess was that Dixon Woods was calling from Afghanistan, using a satellite phone or bouncing through a computer. Either way, if he really wanted to talk, he'd call back.

Sure enough, two minutes later my phone rang again. "Hank Fitch," I said.

Ten seconds later: "Motherfucker . . ."

I hung up again. Instead of the cleaning product I was looking for, I found a five-pound cake of sodium bisulfate, put it in my cart and headed for the electrical department when my phone rang again.

"Hank Fitch," I said.

Ten seconds later: "Do not hang up on me."

"Is this a prank call? I'm a very busy man with no time to listen to obscenity."

"You put my name out. Here I am."

"I put out a lot of names," I said. "Hank Fitch is in the business of putting out names." I didn't even really know what that meant, but I liked the sound of it.

"Dixon Woods," he said.

"Oh," I said. "Yes. The international man of mystery. You put me on the news last night. Something I try to avoid, but then you're not easy to get in contact with. I even drove by your mother's house in Jupiter, but you weren't playing in the front yard."

"Bullshit," he said.

"No bullshit," I said.

"She's dead," he said.

I knew I should have had Sam check her out physically. "You should tell your friend Eddie Champagne that," I said. It didn't really matter, after all. For what I was thinking, she could be dead or alive or stuffed and mounted.

"You think I'm stupid?"

Yes. "No, of course not."

"I know what your guy took from my folder. I know what he knows."

He wasn't stupid. "Here's the deal, Dix," I said. "I'm a businessman. I have certain needs. Needs I sense a person in your unique position could assist me with."

"And what's that position?"

I pushed my cart outside into the garden section. Picked up some new flowers for the front of Cricket's house, a couple pallets of daisies, considered some perennials, something to amp up curb appeal.

"I have a lot of money I want to spend on farm machinery," I said, "and I understand you are in the farming business overseas. Just looking to make a deal."

"Your sense is wrong," Dixon said, but there wasn't much conviction in his voice. The version of Dixon Woods that Eddie Champagne had floated out was too specific not to be based in some kind of truth, too believable to people who can actually do some checking if they have the resources.

"I've got three million dollars I'd like to spend," I said. "I will either spend it with you, or I will spend it with someone else. It's little matter to me. But I figured a person like you, Dixon, with your background, would be able to handle this discreetly. As a token, I will take care of Eddie Champagne permanently for you. You might know that he's been putting your name out there, too. And not always in a flattering fashion. Nevertheless, he told me what I needed to know about you and, drama aside, I was compelled."

Instead of the normal ten-second delay, there was a pause of a full minute, during which time I pulled my cart back inside, took a look at some decorative stone work Lowe's had on display, moved toward the window-treatment aisle.

"I appreciate that," Dixon finally said.

"I'm meeting this week with an old friend from way back east who is spending some time in Miami this month. I'd love for you two to meet, see if we can't find a mutually advantageous business arrangement. Stop worrying about inferior products from Colombia and the like," I said, just to see if Dixon would bite, to see if those little tacks on the map of South Beach meant what I thought they meant.

"I can be on a plane in the morning," Dixon said. "In Miami by tomorrow night."

I picked up a box of solar-powered Malibu lights and tossed them in my cart. A nice touch.

"Call me when you get in," I said.

"Don't worry," Dixon said. "You'll know when I'm in Miami." And then, this time, he hung up.

9

Best-case scenario: You have a plan of attack and everything happens just as it is supposed to. Let's say, for instance, you're waiting for men to arrive with whatever it is you need.

A hostage.

Guns.

Money.

Or maybe it's just a message: The definitive new set of rules that dictate that no one shall make bombs defused by using either a red or blue wire but instead everyone will use the much more easily found black wire and that popular myths of bomb defusion shall reflect said change.

That would be a good message. Helpful to the world. Kids would grow up safer. The terrorists and bad guys and evildoers would lose.

The problem is, most messages, if they're delivered to you personally, end up being bad news. So you learn to prepare for the bad news first. You plan and you counterplan. You devise. You configure. You craft.

You alter.

You mine.

Your best-case scenario ends up being that you've prepared the perfect trap and you end up not needing to use it at all. James Bond, he never had a plan. He had gadgets some research-and-development team would have needed decades to perfect. Jason Bourne? A robot in human skin. Every spy you've ever seen on TV or in a movie has the benefit of special effects—when it gets down to business, all you really have is your plan and your ability to throw it out the window and react to circumstance, deal with consequence, keep fighting.

Or, as I first learned: You either follow tradecraft or you create it.

I didn't fully understand that credo then, but now, when all I can depend on is what I can find myself, it's never made more sense.

Which is why Fiona was in Cricket's garage making tear gas.

Which is why Sam was planting solar-paneled Malibu lights under the windows of Cricket's window . . . and then running fuses from them to tiny explosive squibs under the dirt. Tomorrow, if things went according to plan, those Malibu lights would deliver Fiona's tear gas.

Which is why Cricket O'Connor was standing on her circular staircase watching as Nate and I dragged in new furniture.

Appearances are important, so I asked Nate if it would be possible for him to find some nice furniture we could borrow for a few hours. When he demurred, I mentioned the truck full of men's suits. And now there was a living room filled with furniture.

"Do I want to know where you got this stuff?" I asked. We'd just dragged in a love seat, and Nate was hanging a circular mirror above the fireplace.

"Probably not," Nate said.

I lifted up the cushion on the love seat. I found just under a dollar in change, a takeout menu for a Thai restaurant and a *High School Musical* DVD. "Tell me this wasn't in a kids' room."

"It wasn't in a kids' room."

"A lot of adults watching *High School Musical* these days, Nate?"

"Yes, for your information."

I pulled the DVD out and handed it to Nate. "You're responsible for getting this back to its rightful owner. Can I trust you on that?"

"Sure, bro, sure."

I caught my breath and looked at what Nate and I had assembled. A love seat, another sofa, some pillows, enough to make the place look lived in again.

"Any problem if someone bleeds on the rest of this stuff?" I asked.

"Not from my point of view."

"What about the point of view of the owners?"

"Lot of empty houses around these days," Nate said. "Subprime loans that went upside down. Snowbirds. Easy pickings."

"How do you know about subprime loans?"

"I've got a TV. I read the newspaper," Nate said. "You know, while you were off not stopping terrorism from entering our shores, I did learn how to read."

"Comics don't count. Or your horoscope."

"The word is *astrology*," Nate said.

"Whatever," I said. "I'll try not to get any blood on anything."

"I do you a favor, you could say thank you."

He was right. It's hard for me to say thank you. I'm learning, still. "I appreciate it, Nate," I said. "I really do. With a gold star on top for best behavior. How's that?"

"Just what I wanted to hear," Nate said. "If you'd like something you see, I could probably arrange to get you a few pieces for your place after all of this is up."

"I'm more of a minimalist," I said. I pointed at the mirror. "It's crooked."

Nate looked at it one way. Looked at it another. "Don't see it," he said.

"Trust me," I said. "It's about a half an inch off on the right."

"It's not permanent."

I went over and readjusted the mirror.

"Now it is crooked," Nate said and he went over and pushed it the other direction.

This went on for a couple minutes, until Cricket said from above, "It's fine, Mr. Westen."

"See?" Nate said.

"She was talking to me," I said.

"Why, because she said *Mr.*? You do that all the time, thinking people don't respect me. I'm here doing a job just like you are," Nate said. "A guy could learn to resent his brother really quick."

"Learn?" I said.

And so it went for another few moments, until Sam, who I hadn't see enter the room, but who nonetheless was standing in the entry hall between the kitchen and the living room holding a band of copper wiring, cleared his throat. When I turned and saw him, I also saw Cricket, who by this time looked even more stricken than usual and was standing beside Sam.

"I'm sorry," I said to Cricket. "Family."

"I know," she said. "I'm not upset about that. I'm upset that I don't have that anymore. You two arguing reminds me of my son and his father. You two have a real shorthand, even when you're angry or frustrated. You only find that with people who love each other. I guess I should have recognized that sooner."

I understood and said so. "Nate," I said, "I don't think you've been properly introduced. This is Cricket O'Connor. She's the person we're helping here. Cricket, this is my brother, Nate Westen. He's kindly found us some furniture to use for the day."

Nate wiped his hands off on his pants, then apologized for wiping his hands off on his pants, and then finally just walked up and shook Cricket's hand. "I'm sorry for your loss," he said, as if he were at a funeral for someone he didn't know, which, in a way, he was. We all were.

"Of what?" Cricket said.

"Of everything," Nate said.

Cricket smiled wanly at Nate. "I appreciate your help," she said. "It's not for me, though."

Nate looked at her quizzically, so I stepped in before he could speak any more. "I haven't explained everything to Nate," I said. I ran down the basics.

"Why haven't you just found this asshole and shot him?" Nate asked when I finished.

"What good would it do for those families Cricket is supporting if I kill him, Nate? How does that make me any better than he is? This is about getting back what's been taken and using it for the right reasons."

"I get it," Nate said, "though you have to admit it would be awfully satisfying to shoot him."

Everyone agreed that was true, including, much to my surprise, Cricket. That, too, would pass. If everything went according to plan, or even if it didn't, Cricket would still have her own heartache to deal with. The difference between love and hate isn't so severe when you're in the thick of either emotion and I did realize by then one important thing: Though Cricket had been bamboozled, had lost everything, really, she still felt something for the man who swept her off her feet, even if it was a lie. I thought about the photos Fiona and I saw of them at that benefit. Thought about how happy Cricket looked. How as she and Eddie Champagne walked into that party they looked like real people, like people you'd see in a magazine and imagine had the most perfect life, people you'd wish you were.

Your life is never as rich as what other people presume it is or, often, what you believe it is. It happened to Cricket with her first husband, too, which made it all the worse. But I guess it happens to all of us, eventually: We lose track of what it was we thought we were doing with ourselves, and one day, we wake up, and we are in a fix beyond our control.

Cricket O'Connor got her own burn notice.

I'd try to make it right for one of us.

Bullies never take on anyone they can't beat. That's what makes them predictable. You want to find a coward? Remove all forms of inevitability. Change circumstances. Introduce unusual danger.

Or, barring that, know how to make tear gas.

Everything you need can be found at Home Depot or Lowe's, or, if you live in a city that has a Super Wal-Mart, you can get all your tear gas ingredients at the same time you purchase a rifle, the entire first season of *The Love Boat* on DVD and clothes made by Malaysians. And since 9/11, they even carry gas masks now, too. Bulk shopping at its best: entertainment, fashion, terrorism and safety all in one place.

Guns are easy until you have to use one. In the history of combat, before we started desensitizing our soldiers and happily allowed them to return home mentally neutered, traditionally only 15 percent of the people tasked with shooting another person were actually able to do it. There's a reason why firing squads were used for decades—most of the shooters will miss out of simple human nature. But if you aren't sure you're the person who provided the kill shot, it's much easier to go through life without putting another bullet in your own head.

Tear gas, on the other hand, has no moral component.

Nor does Fiona when it comes to making weapons.

"If you gave me a bit more time," Fiona said, "I could make a batch of mustard gas."

"That's all right," I said. "No reason to take down the whole island." Fiona and I were in Cricket's garage mixing up a usable sum of tear gas to use for personal consumption. And by personal, I mean I was going to take great personal glee in using it on the people shaking Cricket down, who, I was beginning to suspect, were far from real bad guys. Real bad guys don't just keep coming back for more money like their mark is an ATM machine or the newest fish in a pyramid scheme.

Real bad guys would expect someone like Cricket to go to the police. Real bad guys would have killed Cricket. Real bad guys didn't give a shit about people like Eddie Champagne, because a real bad guy would know a guy as sloppy and stupid as I was beginning to see Eddie was could never be someone like Dixon Woods. Dixon Woods wasn't stupid. Dixon Woods wasn't sloppy. Dixon Woods might be a bad guy, he might be a good guy, but what he wasn't was a fool.

Tomorrow, I'd see if I could work around that.

"Too bad," Fiona said. She'd set up a workstation in Cricket's garage and was now running a length of rubber tubing outside to a hose spigot. "Clamp this," she said when she returned and handed me one end of the tube and what looked like a jam jar. She moved around behind me, her hand sliding across my back, and stood beside me again, and started measuring out the sodium bisulfate. She worked delicately with the compound, cutting and sizing while I fixed together a series of tubes and ad hoc beakers, using mostly things we'd cleaned out of Cricket's cabinets and refrigerator.

The problem with using things like peanut butter and jelly jars instead of sanitized lab equipment is that you can never be sure what's been left behind. A little peanut oil can mean a lot of fire. And when you're making tear gas, a lot of fire is not, patently, a good thing.

"Careful," I said. Fiona was about to mix the sodium bisulfate with glycerin soap—not the perfect recipe for tear gas, but one that will do in a pinch, or when you can't find a craft store that has the purest stuff. Fortunately, Cricket had plenty of very good soap, and very good soap is what you need if you want to make tear gas in the garage of your mansion.

"Careful, yourself," Fiona said. "You should stand back. I'm going to heat this now."

I moved closer to her.

A weird thing happens between Fiona and me when we make weapons.

It's not sexual in the physical sense, but it certainly

is mentally. There is a quality of excitement when you know you're working on something lethal with someone who understands what lethal really means. It's more than shared experience, of course, because if it were, I'd find Sam equally attractive. You spend your life feinting from things that can hurt you or you dive headlong, there is no middle ground, and so when you find someone who shares a chemical disposition toward immersion . . . and if she happens to casually roll against you in ways that make you think of the sex you imagined before you ever had sex . . . even when you're wearing gas masks, which, at the moment, we were . . . well, you keep them in your life, even if it's ultimately bad for your health.

"If we are both permanently disfigured," I said, "we'll still have each other."

"Enticing," Fiona said and then she mixed the sodium bisulfate and soap together without incident. We spent the next several minutes hip to hip, finger to finger, breath to breath (albeit in gas masks), capturing gas into rubber-stopped glass vials.

It was the best date I'd been on in a long, long time.

When we were done, we washed off using the hose on the side of the yard so we wouldn't bring any residual chemicals into the house. Even I couldn't disregard how bizarre things sometimes were between us.

"What are you smiling about?" Fi asked.

"This," I said. "You and me. Giving each other a hose shower after making tear gas."

"It's not the strangest thing."

"No," I said. "No, it's not."

"It could be a lot worse, Michael. You could be searching for women on the Internet."

"That would be worse." We hadn't heard from Eddie through Fiona's profile yet, but I had a feeling today would be the day. Call it intuition. Call it knowing that Eddie Champagne was about to have a cash-flow problem. Call it by any name you want, but what's great about bullies, even weak ones, is that they are predictable, and, if you know what you're doing, you can plan for things they don't even know they're about to think.

I turned off the hose and Fi and I toweled off using a few of Cricket's guest towels, which must have had an insanely high thread count, since even Fi sort of paused and rubbed it along her cheek.

"You could be in a situation like Cricket's," I said.

"Oh, that wouldn't be so bad," she said. "I could get used to this house. These towels. A Bentley or two. I might even take up badminton."

"A couple weeks in a place like this, you'd be robbing banks again."

"You don't know, Michael. I might really enjoy hitting the shuttlecock." I laughed. It felt pretty good. "Of course, I'd have to give up meaningful moments like this with you."

"I don't know, Fi. You're right about that," I said, "though I might be inclined to look you up online eventually, see if you were interested in former spies looking for a good home."

"It wouldn't be a good home," Fiona said. She was close to me now, as close as we'd been making the tear gas. "You'd be gone before I would be."

"Maybe."

"And there'd always be someone like Natalya for you to worry about."

"Who said I was worried?"

Fiona patted my chest and then left her hand there, her fingers pressing and releasing. "You're human, Michael, even if you swear you're not."

"Fi," I said.

"I know. I know. I saw the movie, too."

"Which one was that?"

"Bad man. Bad woman. Bad things happen and then the woman inevitably is left to pine away for her dark man. And then he comes back, someone smirks and it's a happy ending. Always so stupid. You'd think one day someone would call for a little authenticity. All the endings I've been part of have been unhappy, if you want the truth, if it involves bad men and bad women."

Fiona was smiling now, aware of her moment, probably thinking, *Yeah, now I've got Michael pondering how mundane we've made these things. They even make movies about it. . . .*

"What is that, *The Maltese Falcon*?"

Smile still there, but a little angry now. These games we play, they're fun. They are. But at base, she's a woman, I'm a man and we're always about one reflex away from platonic going erotic. "The point is, Michael, I already know the why. It doesn't change things, because here we are."

"Don't tell me it was a Bond film. Those things make me crazy." Above us, a plane was making its descent into Miami, the airport only a few miles away from Fisher Island, but another world away in every other sense. The buzzing of the engine caught Fiona's attention, too, and for a moment we both just watched the plane as it banked slightly to the east to start its circle down. When it was gone from overhead, I looked down at Fiona. She was beautiful. Is beautiful. And yet. And yet. "You ever wonder, Fi, about what else is out there for you."

"I've told you before, Michael, I know what's out there. It's not compelling."

"This is? Whatever we have here?"

"It's better."

"Maybe you'll die because it was better. That ever occur to you?"

"You wouldn't let that happen, now, would you, Michael?"

I wanted to kiss her. I really did.

"No, I suppose I wouldn't. Aren't you lucky. Did I tell you Natalya called you my pit bull?"

"Failed to mention that."

"I thought you'd like that," I said.

I had a really good sense Fiona wanted to kiss me, too. It was the way she was pressing herself into me, the way I was intimately aware of the word *pelvis*.

"She call me any other names?"

"Not that I recall," I said.

Things were moving at a pace I wasn't entirely comfortable with, but which were nonetheless acquiring their own velocity. I put a hand on Fiona's clavicle and gently pushed her backward. "You need to get out of here," I said. I checked my watch. It was four thirty. I wanted Fiona back at my mother's, just in a case any more Communists showed up. Sam and Nate needed to leave me and Cricket alone, at least for a little while.

"Of course I do," she said, that smile back again. She finally stepped away from me, though I could still feel her fingers on my chest, other parts of her on other parts of me. "That's what makes it compelling, Michael. You're the only man who can push a woman away even when you know it would be a good time."

"I can't be the only one," I said.

"The only one I care about," Fiona said.

10

Here's how a shakedown works: You scare someone so badly by threatening them that they actually believe paying you is better than going to the police, because they figure if you have the brass to threaten someone with impunity, you must have impunity. You scare someone to the point that everything they've ever learned goes out the window and they just rely on that fight-or-flight impulse, except that instead of running away, they cower. They submit.

In Cricket's case, her shakedown came far easier. Eddie Champagne, who I was looking forward to taking a little bubbly out of, probably read about her first. Knew enough about her from the newspaper and magazine stories that he could pinch himself into her life and shake her without fear. There was no Dixon Woods to show up in the middle of the night and slap him around. The only impediment was going to be time and knowledge: Time for his past to find him, time for Cricket to wise up. So it didn't surprise me that he had disappeared when he did.

Or that Barry recognized him.

Or that as soon as he disappeared from Cricket's life, someone else showed up to collect.

Or that he thought he might need guns at some point.

I explained this very thought process to Cricket as we sat in her living room—her newly adorned living room—waiting for her bad guys to float up to her dock. I needed to make sure the men who came to collect were the same men as always. If they were, I'd know Eddie was none the wiser. I told her she didn't need to be afraid anymore, because whoever those men were, they had nothing on me. That she should be calm now. That I was in control. But it didn't stop her from looking panicked.

"I understand that all intellectually," she said, "but they scare me."

"Trust me," I said.

Twenty minutes later, a Power Quest zipped up to Cricket's dock. It was an expensive model, the 340 Vyper, and it looked new. I counted three men on the boat. The most marked characteristic I picked out about all three was that they tucked their shirts into their shorts and that they were wearing what looked like orthopedic sandals, the kind with the straps that wrap around the ankle and have extra padding to fight against aggressive cases of plantar fasciitis. They looked like the kind of guys who took lunch at that one strip club with the afternoon buffet. I put all three of them at no older than forty. I put their weights down as no less than 250, and that wasn't muscle weight or water retention. That was cheese-and-beef weight. In their free time, when they weren't shaking down women, I suspected they sat on that boat together and listened to the Jimmy Buffett box set and told one another lies.

What they weren't, categorically, was dangerous.

I asked Cricket if these were the same three guys who always collected from her. She said yes. Sam was waiting for her down the drive, but before I let her leave, I asked, "And what scares you about them?"

"They threatened to kill me," she said.

"If they killed you," I said, "they wouldn't get any more money out of you. If they killed Dixon, same deal."

Cricket thought about that. "I never considered that," she said.

"I know. That's why you can trust me. Okay?" I watched the men walk from the dock and across to the grasscrete pathway that circled around the numerous estates and led up from the personal marinas. Sam is waiting on the other side of your gate in your car. I'm going to take care of this. If you hear something that sounds like a gunshot while you're walking, don't be concerned."

"What does a gunshot sound like?"

"You'll know," I said.

The sun was already halfway down when Cricket scurried away. Outside, Biscayne Bay looked flat and glassy. I could make out a FOSS tanker coming into port. Overhead, planes were taxiing into and out of Miami International. Next door, in another multimillion dollar mansion, I suspected people were probably eating dinner. It would be a lobster bisque kind of night—just cool enough once the sun disappeared that you'd catch a chill. Dixon Woods, the real Dixon Woods, was making calls right now—I was sure of that—trying to figure out who Hank Fitch was. Brenda Holcomb was explaining just what the hell had happened in the offices of Longstreet Security. Natalya Choplyn was likely plotting how to kill me. My own government was working on that issue, too. My mother was smoking. My father was rotting in the ground, and though there was plenty of space in the cemetery, I had no desire to join him.

I checked my gun. Made sure the silencer was on just right.

I cracked my neck, because I'd slept funny the night previous.

I thought about Fiona and her hand on my chest.

I called Sam. "They're here," I said. "Cricket's on her way. Give me ten minutes. Text me when you're on your way back up."

This? This was going to be fun.

Because there's fight.

There's flight.

There's submission.

And then there's posture. You see this in the wild all the time. You watch the Discovery Channel long enough, you'll find out that every animal from the cocker spaniel to the black bear and all points above and below strike a pose. How you pose. How you stand. How you present yourself makes all the difference when you're about to get into a fight.

You assess the danger and you pose accordingly.

When I was Jay Gatz, my pose was all money and privilege and never taking no for an answer.

When I was the guy asking for directions to the airport, I was an idiot the security guard shouldn't have turned his back on.

Hank Fitch? His pose was simple. A guy you simply do not want to fuck with.

I watched the three men make their way around the house, watched as they smiled and slapped backs and got themselves mentally prepared to be bad asses and decided that I'd shoot the happiest-looking one of the bunch if I had the choice, but any of them would do. Through the peephole, I could see them adjusting their pants, making sure their shirts were tucked in just right.

It was like watching three high school buddies heading to the whorehouse for the first time, each getting the other up for their two minutes of glory.

The fattest of the three, a guy wearing a blue polo shirt with a penguin logo on it, pounded on the door and actually bellowed, "Open up!"

I swung open the door. "Yeah?" I said. I kept my gun hand behind the door.

The three guys looked at one another with varying degrees of surprise and annoyance. I'd dressed down for the occasion, so instead of wearing a suit, I had on a pair of jeans and a black T-shirt that made me look sort of like a college professor on his day off, except that behind the door instead of holding a sheaf of student papers, I was holding a Russian 6P9, an eight-round silenced pistol. A gift from Fiona.

"Who are you?" Blue Shirt said. His buddies, Striped Shirt and Yellow Shirt, tried to look intimidating. It wasn't working. It's hard to look intimidating when you're wearing a rope belt, which all three of them were.

"Hank Fitch," I said. "Who are you?"

"We're here for Cricket," Striped Shirt said.

"Then you're in the right place," I said, all downhome goodness. "Come on in. She's in the living room." I opened the door wide and the three men walked into the entry hall, single file. Yellow Shirt actually gave me a polite nod, like maybe I was just the houseboy there to help out for the day, and he was just another guy at the end of his work day.

I could have shot each of them in the back of the head before a single one of them had a moment to react. Instead, as they walked by, I did a cursory once-over again, just to see if there were any bulges in odd places, apart from their guts. All three had cell phones clipped to their belts, while Striped Shirt had an ancient-looking revolver shoved down the front of his shorts. This would be fun.

Blue Shirt and Striped Shirt had wedding rings. Yellow Shirt had a wedding ring and one of those bulky class rings. I had a feeling it wasn't from the Citadel.

All three were wearing Rolexes.

I followed them into the living room, where all three were standing around looking lost. Everything in the room was different, right down to the window shades and pictures. I had my hands behind my back in a courtly pose that I figured would make the fact that I had a gun in my hand less apparent, not that these three had much in terms of cognitive resonance.

"What's going on here?" Blue Shirt said. "Where's Cricket?"

"New rules," I said.

"Yeah?" Blue Shirt said.

"Yeah," I said, and to prove it, I pulled out my gun. In most cases, pulling out a gun is enough to stop someone from acting stupid. They recognize that you have a gun and they decide they'll cut through their bullshit mechanisms and act rationally—which is to say, they'll cower in fear. Unfortunately, Striped Shirt thought the appearance of my gun was an invitation for him to draw his Civil War relic and attempt to shoot me.

The first problem he encountered was that he'd never shot anyone before. The second problem is that in the space of time it took him to realize he didn't know what the hell he was doing, I grabbed his gun hand and then pistol-whipped him, which is like getting hit in the face with a slab of very accurate metal. I broke his nose and took out at least five teeth, maybe more if he swallowed a couple, but five was what was left on the ground.

This didn't stop Yellow Shirt from trying to come

at me from behind, which would have been a problem if Striped Shirt didn't squeeze off a round at the same moment (I doubted it was intentional, but involuntary things happen when you're writhing in pain), hitting his partner in the leg. It was all over in about five seconds and I didn't even need to personally shoot anyone.

I gently removed the gun from Striped Shirt's hand and emptied the bullets into my pocket while Blue Shirt just sort of stared at me.

"Here," I said, and handed the gun to Blue Shirt, who shoved it wordlessly into his cargo shorts. I decided to let Blue Shirt be the one to make sense of it all, since one of them had to be alert. "I'd hate for your friend to lose such a priceless heirloom."

If you get shot in the leg, here's what happens: The bullet enters your leg, which hurts, and then, if it hits the bone, the odds are the bone will shatter, which also hurts. The shattered fragments of bone will scatter around inside your leg or out the back, if the bullet doesn't get lodged in the muscle.

What does *hurt* feel like?

It feels like someone has detonated a bomb inside of you. It feels like someone has replaced your blood with hot gravel. It feels like you're about to die. Because you'll actually be suffering from three wounds: the entry wound, the percussion wounds from the bullet pinging around your bone, and the exit wound. You'll probably flop on your back and then black out. When you awake, which could be just a few seconds later, you'll probably cry. People who get shot tend to cry.

If you think you're going to get shot, tell your two buddies who think they're tough guys—but who really haven't had any experience with this kind of conflict, who have only seen people shot on television and in video games, because if you run around with two buddies, the odds are you play video games—to eat a light lunch, too. Get shot in the leg in front of your two buddies, and as soon as they are showered by bits of bone, skin, muscle, and maybe a little bit of your orthopedic sandals, the odds are they're going to dry heave.

If you want to go into a field of business where people will get shot around you, or where you might get shot, it's a nice idea to strengthen your gag reflex.

After Blue Shirt and Striped Shirt stopped gagging, Striped Shirt on the perfect mixture of his own blood and a nice sum of his own teeth, I gave a whistle to get their attention. "Gentlemen," I said, "unless you want your friend to bleed to death, you might want to apply a tourniquet to his leg." Blue Shirt looked at me blankly. Striped Shirt was still trying to catch his breath, which was hard because his face was broken in half. Yellow Shirt? He was moaning and crying and trying to crawl away, which wasn't working too well because he had a shattered shinbone. The truth was that he was unlikely to bleed to death anytime soon, but it wouldn't hurt to stanch the bleeding lest he slip into shock from blood loss and go into cardiac arrest. "What's your name?" I said to Blue Shirt. I had the gun on him, which I think got him to focus.

"Stan," he said. His voice was weak and scared, which was the point, after all.

"Stan, I want you to take off that rope belt you have holding up your shorts, and I want you to bind it tight across your friend's shin."

Stan yanked his belt off and did just that. Striped Shirt, at this point, was a useless mess. He was curled against the wall beneath the mirror and was sort of mumbling and whimpering. He'd need plastic surgery if he ever wanted to model. He was sputtering now, coughing, gagging some more.

"Tell your friend over there to lean forward, or else he's going to choke on his own blood," I said to Stan. "If he leans forward, it will drain."

Stan repeated what I'd just said, which actually got Striped Shirt to move. "You killed my brother-in-law," Striped Shirt managed to say once he was able to cough out some blood. He meant, I presumed, the guy he actually shot.

"I didn't kill anyone yet," I said. "If he's still bleeding, that means he's still alive. That's how that works." I leaned down and looked at Yellow Shirt's wound. It was a good one, but he'd live. He'd limp for the rest of his life, but he'd have a good story to tell, replete with a moral and everything.

"Stan," I said, "you'll note I haven't hurt you yet. So let's get something straight."

"Anything," he said.

"As you can see," I said, "Cricket is no longer with us. Whatever debt you think she owed you? That's gone."

"We just collect," Stan said. He was looking back and forth at his two friends, like he couldn't believe what he was seeing, like he'd never imagined a situation in his life where he'd be surrounded by that much blood. Faces and legs tend to gush.

"Of course you do," I said. "Now let's be straight here, gentlemen, before I have to shoot someone else. Would I be correct in saying you work for Dixon Woods?"

"I don't even know who Dixon Woods is, man," the shot guy spit out. He was rather lucid now, despite the gunshot wound, the pain, the tourniquet, the likely realization he was having that he'd have to explain to his wife how he get shot. "I've been shot for some motherfucker I don't even know. I'm having trouble seeing. Jesus. I'm going fucking blind over here."

"You should know your clients better," I said. "What kind of organization sends three men to collect from a woman? You need to talk to your boss, gentlemen, get a better idea of the dangers involved. Maybe see if he'll spring for some shooting lessons. A lesson would be a good thing to have had right now, wouldn't it, Stan?"

"No, sir," Stan said.

"We can be honest with each other, Stan," I said. "Let me guess, you just like to slap women around. Is that right, Stan?"

"No, sir," he said again.

"What about you?" I said to Yellow Shirt, whose yellow shirt was now covered completely in sweat. It did look like he was suffering.

"I'm going blind," Yellow Shirt said again.

"That's from pain and blood loss," I said. I turned to Stan. "What exactly do you do for a living, Stan?"

"What?" He was starting to get glassy-eyed, too. Slipping into shock and nothing had even happened to him. That can happen when you're in combat: You see someone get shot in front of you, it has a life-affirming effect or it has a life-stunting effect. On Stan, it seemed the latter. The one with the broken face had fallen oddly silent, too, apart from the crying and this weird sucking sound he was making through his missing teeth.

"Do you have a job, Stan? Something that allows you the opportunity to leave work early on a Thursday to shake down socialites?"

"We sell real estate," he said.

"See, that's interesting," I said. "Because you know what I do?" Stan shook his head. He was starting to look a little clammy. "I invest. Take a look around, Stan. What do you see?"

Stan looked around. "Furniture," he said.

"What kind of furniture, Stan?"

"Nice stuff," he said.

"That's right. What else? Look outside. Go ahead. Stand up. What do you see?"

Stan got up, looked outside the window, saw the new flowers. The decorative stones. The Malibu lights, which weren't armed yet, because a guy needs to keep his surprises to a minimum sometimes. The trimmed lawn. I even had the fountain going. "You've taken care of the garden again," he said. "Made it look nice."

"Right again," I said. "You see, Stan, while you were busy shaking Cricket down for your boss—and we'll get to that in one second, Stan, because I can see you're starting to get nervous that maybe I didn't believe your friend's assertion that he didn't know Dixon—I was looking at the big picture from a boss' perspective. Saw a real business opportunity here. You three are just bagmen. But I like Dixon's moxie here, pimping his own wife. That's a class operation. So you know what I did? I bought the house."

I pointed the gun at Stan when I said this, let him know I really meant what I said. I didn't of course. At least not exactly.

"Look," Stan said, "don't shoot me."

"I'm not going to shoot you, Stan," I said. "Whatever gave you that impression?"

"You shot Burl," he said, pointing to the man on the ground. I didn't bother to correct his error. If he thought I shot his friend, all the better.

"Why don't you just tell him all of our names!" Burl said. "Give him your social security number while you're at it, Stan! Jesus. I'm having trouble breathing."

"If you were really having trouble breathing," I said, "you wouldn't be able to talk." I looked over at the fellow under the mirror, the one who would need some real dental care if he hoped to chew anything ever again. The upshot is that I might have fixed any deviated septum issues he might have had. "What's his name, Stan?"

"Danny," he said.

"Okay," I said. "Stan, Burl, Danny, here's the deal: I know you're working for Dixon. I don't hold that against you. But Dixon and I have a business interest overseas that he's reneged on recently. It took me a very long time to find him, so I was fortunate when I finally met Ms. O'Connor and learned of her problems. She's graciously allowed me to move into her home, which I've happily done. The real problem, the one you three are paying the price for here, is that your employer Dixon owes me a substantial amount of money, gentlemen. So I want you to get him a message. Are you listening?"

Stan, Burl and even Danny, all regarded me with expectant looks.

"I'm not concerned about the opium anymore. The price of doing business." All three men darted looks at one another. If I had an idea about Eddie Champagne, it was that even the people working for him, in this case three real estate agents, were probably suspicious of his background, but not all that willing to be too suspicious if money kept flowing to them. Now that one of them had been shot, opium farms in Afghanistan probably seemed like a real possibility. I figured if I tossed in *the price of doing business* as a mysterious rejoinder, well, they'd figure getting shot was the price, too.

At any rate, I had their attention.

"What I can't forgive," I continued, "is the mess he left me with in California. That ended up costing me a great deal of money and resulted in the Mexican Mafia putting a hit order on me, which you can imagine didn't please me." Now I was just riffing, adding on, letting Stan, Burl and Danny know they were in deep with someone they didn't even know, someone who might end up rolling a hit onto them.

Guys like Hank Fitch can deal with a La Eme.

Stan, Burl and Danny? They watched documentaries on *Dateline* about that sort of thing and felt claustrophobic with fear, as if watching the program might mark them as snitches and result in a shank in their granite-lined showers while their wives pressed their morning espresso.

Eddie Champagne? If he knew Dixon Woods had a problem with the Mexican Mafia, Eddie would ditch his name and his holdings and any money he thought anyone might associate with it and get out of town quickly. (Out of the country if he could, but I had Sam working on that.)

"But this new real estate business Dixon is in I find very compelling," I said. "I can't imagine it's on the level. Is it, Stan?"

"Mr. Fitch . . . ," he started.

"Hank," I said. "We're friends. Call me Hank."

"Whatever you had with Mr. Woods before today, we weren't aware of that," Stan said.

"There it goes," Burl said. "We're fucking dead. Do you get that, Stan? We're fucking dead. Danny, we're fucking dead."

"You," I said to Burl, "quiet." I pointed the gun at him when I spoke, which was a mistake, because he immediately pissed himself. There was now piss and blood on the floor. Fortunately, the furniture looked pretty good. I was keeping the exchange of fluids pretty well contained to the fireplace region.

"Continue," I said to Stan.

"I want to help you close this deal," he said, like we were sitting in the front seat of his BMW talking about a house in a subdivision. "All I know, all my associates know, is the business end. Dixon tells us where the money is, we get it, we make it happen. All this drug stuff? That's not us."

"Of course it isn't," I said. I smiled, just to let Stan know I understood, let him know that this was all just a big misunderstanding. "You just come around and fleece defenseless women—is that right, Stan? Pretend to be a tough guy? Make a woman lose her house to a guy like me? Make her a fucking shell of a human? That what you do?"

Stan looked nervously at his two friends. "Well, it's . . ."

"It's what I say it is," I said.

"Yes, sir," Stan said.

"What about you, Burl?" I said.

"I can't feel my foot," Burl said.

"That's because you've been shot in the leg, and no blood is making it to your foot right now," I said. I was about to ask Danny, the guy in the striped shirt, if he agreed, too, but he still didn't look like he could be engaged in conversation.

"You were saying, Stan?"

"The problem, as I see it," Stan said, "is that in order for me to help you with your plans, it would be helpful if we could cut Dixon out of it. No need to have him involved, respectfully, if you're interested in getting into this market."

I had to hand it to Stan. He was a good real estate agent.

"Go ahead," I said.

"We have relationships in place already," Stan said. He rattled off the names of several high-profile banks where he had *contacts* and where he said he ran millions of dollars in silly loans daily. What he outlined was a nice criminal enterprise of faulty loans that no one would know about unless, well, unless the banks started paying attention, which I had a feeling was about to happen. Soon enough, if you watched the news, you knew everyone working in real estate would get caught, even the legit companies. "We could bring you into the fold. Get you started locally. Avoid all this crap with Dixon. This island? It's gold, Mr. Fitch." He explained that over the last year they'd become very adept at getting loans on properties all over Miami for far more than the property was worth, that they'd paid the right people using Dixon's connections and reputation and that it was now a flawless clockwork operation.

"We could use a person with your . . . flair . . . Mr. Fitch, to really take this to the next level."

"That's very generous," I said, though I wasn't

precisely certain what it meant. But I had a feeling Barry might. "And in return?"

"You make sure Dixon doesn't kill us," he said, "or have his people hurt our families. You seem like the kind of person who could help with that."

His people. The only people Eddie Champagne had were probably living in a trailer in Sarasota, hoping to get bitten by a gator on state land so they could sue.

Hank Fitch, however, was precisely that kind of guy.

Still, I had to hand it to Stan. In the face of adversity, he managed to bring his A game, negotiation-wise. He almost had me believing that this was all an excellent idea. But one had to admire a guy who could negotiate a deal to save his ass and get a new, meaner, more obviously psychotic business partner. Stan wouldn't make a bad warlord.

"There'd still be the matter then of the debt Dixon owes me," I said.

"We could cover that debt," Stan said.

"It's sizable," I said. I told him it was five million dollars. I figured that would cover all of my bases.

"We could cover that debt," Stan said, though he swallowed perceptibly.

"Wired," I said.

"Wired," Stan said.

"By tomorrow," I said.

"I don't know if—"

"By tomorrow," I said.

"By tomorrow," Stan said.

I extended my hand and Stan shook it. "You have a deal, Stan," I said. My cell chirped and I saw a text from Sam. Everything was working better than I could have possibly hoped for. "There's something I want you to see." I stepped Stan over to the window so he could see Sam drive up and park Cricket's Mercedes. Sam was behind the wheel. Cricket was in the passenger seat. And Nate was sitting in the back.

"You see those two men with Cricket?" Stan nodded. "You don't seem like a bad guy, Stan. And neither do your friends."

"Thank you," he said, because I think he thought that life was just getting easier and easier.

"But I am," I said. "You screw me? Those men are going to kill Cricket. There's nothing you'll be able to do to stop it. And you might notice that you've touched quite a bit of stuff in this room, Stan. Fingerprints everywhere. A good amount of blood and piss too. Let's not forget motive. You watch *CSI*, Stan?"

"Sometimes," he said.

"Watch it this week. See if anyone leaves that much evidence around anymore," I said. "Do you hear me?"

"I hear you," he said.

I waved at Sam to let him know he could drive off.

"Today," I said, "you go back to Dixon and tell him Cricket was gone. Tell him everything that happened here, if you like, except for the deal you've graciously made me. Tell him his money supply is gone. Tell him I'm looking for him. Tell him I'm right here, waiting. Understand?"

Stan said he did.

"You'll make sure your friends understand?" I said. Burl had fallen silent, the pain finally overriding the adrenaline and knocking him out. Danny? He was pulling bits of blood, flesh and teeth off of his shirt.

"Yes, sir, Mr. Fitch," Stan said.

"Do you have a business card, Stan?"

"Pardon me?"

"A business card. Something with your firm name on it? A way to contact you?"

"Oh, right," Stan said. He motioned to his back pocket. "I'm going to pull out my wallet, just so you know."

"Got it," I said. At least he was learning not to make any rash movements.

Stan rummaged through his wallet and came out with a gold-embossed card that said his name was Stanley Rosencrantz. What kind of guy named Stanley Rosencrantz would possibly think this was a way to conduct business? Stanley Rosencrantz should have been sitting behind a desk somewhere, permanently, his ass growing exponentially larger each day. His firm was called White Rose Partners. How friendly.

"Nice card," I said.

"We can get you one, too," he said. Now he was just babbling. "Whatever you want."

"I'll have an account set up tomorrow for the wire. You'll have the money ready."

"Tomorrow is a little early," he said.

"If you are who you think you are," I said, "you can have this done in forty minutes. I'm giving you until tomorrow as a courtesy, since you're going to need to take your friends to the hospital, figure out a way to lie to everyone you know, maybe get a script for some Xanax to get yourself asleep tonight, kiss your wife goodbye in case it turns out that I kill you anyway."

"I—"

"Tomorrow, Stan. Tomorrow."

"Tomorrow," he said.

I stepped to one side, offering Stan a path around me. "Then by all means," I said, "get to work. And a word about your friends. You might want to avoid a regular hospital. I'm not sure you want to be talking to the police, Stan. Maybe go across to Little Haiti. Find a nice clinic, throw around some money, hope no one forgets to sterilize their surgical implements. Hate to have your friends die of an infection, after all they've been through."

Stan nodded, but didn't move. He was going to need to talk to someone about post-traumatic shock, but I figured I'd let him figure that out. "Do you have a card?" Stan asked finally, "some way for me to call you?"

"Did Dixon have a card, Stan?"

"Well, yes," he said.

Eddie Champagne really was an idiot.

"That's why I'm not Dixon Woods," I said. "When you think you need to contact me, I'll have already contacted you." That sounded ominous enough. I let it sink in. "Now, Stan? Get the fuck out of my house."

11

If you live in Miami and need to make millions and millions of dollars in a short period of time, but have no discernible skills that would allow you to either play quarterback for the Dolphins, first base for the Marlins or, with Shaq out of the picture, center for the Heat, you have three choices:

1. You can deal drugs. This is a good choice. Miami has a large transient population of Hollywood and New York types who like to ingest as much cocaine as possible over the course of a weekend and won't haggle over price. Miami also has a disproportionately large refugee population, which, while used to huffing glue, has become an equitable buyer of crack, meth and marijuana, as well, which is nice since it's hard to move glue these days. Selling drugs can be dangerous, of course, so if you're concerned about your life or liberty, you could just keep your business confined to the sixteen thousand members of the University of Miami's student body, at least a quarter of

whom like to take some recreational drugs. And then there's the retirees who can't afford the really good Oxycontin or Vicodin on their fixed incomes, so if you had a contact or two in the retirement villages, you could probably make a nice living without ever being threatened at all. You need a million dollars? Get yourself some cocaine or heroin and move to Miami, set up shop, get to work. If you can't make your nut, you're using your own supply.

2. You can marry in. This is a better choice. Even though Miami-Dade County has a median income lower than the rest of the nation, it also has millionaires by the legion. You just need to know where to find them. Fisher Island, of course. Snapper Creek and Hammock Lakes in Coral Gables. Biscayne Park. Cocoplum. The entire stretch of the Keys. If you're a man, this might be slightly more difficult, though not impossible. If you're a woman, if you haven't been seriously deformed in an industrial accident, if your name is Star, or if it used to be, you could live a millionaire's life without any outlay of your own, apart from the cost of your belly-button ring and hair dye.

3. You can go into real estate. This is the best choice. The reason? Because people will give you money for nothing. People will give you money on the idea of land. The presumption of inflation. The chance that they'll be able to turn their own millions of dollars into millions of dollars more. The chance that when you promise them a huge, absurd return on investment—say, 20 or 30 percent—that you are

just the finest real estate investment program in the history of real estate.

Of course, it helps if people think a former Green Beret is running the company, investing his own money in the venture, because an ex–Green Beret must be an honorable man. During this time of war, surely an ex–Green Beret wouldn't be defrauding people out of millions of dollars in fraudulent properties and mortgages.

But then, Eddie Champagne wasn't exactly an ex–Green Beret. Dixon Woods was. Eddie Champagne, not even a raspberry beret. But the people behind White Rose Partners didn't know that. They just knew he had money and reputation and stories. And he had connections to more money. And when things got dicey, when it looked like there might be a problem, well, he had a human ATM in Cricket O'Connor.

What they were running out of was time.

Or at least that's what Sam's source at the IRS told him. After Stan managed to drag his two partners back out to their boat, we got Cricket back to my mother's and let Sam work the phones to find out what he could on White Rose Partners and what more he might find on Eddie Champagne.

One of Sam's sources at the IRS was an investigator named Lenore. Like his source at the FBI, Kyle, Sam had never actually met Lenore face-to-face. But when an ex-girlfriend got into a bit of jam and was facing a potentially hazardous audit—one that would probably show her husband just how much money she'd spent out with Sam—Sam called in a few interagency chits and ended up on the phone with Lenore, who simply hit the DELETE key a couple of times, and Sam's girlfriend's problems disappeared.

Over the years, he'd found that Lenore was one of the more dependable people out there, if only because she never seemed to fall for any of his charms, which Sam found both admirable and baffling. He thought of sending her a photo of himself from his younger, more muscular days, but decided, ultimately, that if she worked for the IRS, she probably knew his financial portfolio pretty well and was sure that, charm-wise, that was a black mark.

Still, he always tried to put a dash of sugar into their conversations. He called her under the aegis of just checking into an investment opportunity, making sure all was legit. A perfectly reasonable thing for someone to do, Sam thought, if one had the connections. But as soon as he brought up the White Rose Partners, he could actually hear her training take over. "I'm going to need to call you back, Samuel," she said abruptly.

She always called him Samuel. She was the only person alive who called him Samuel. But this time it didn't sound remotely affectionate, like it usually did. Fifteen minutes later, she called him from a secure conference line, which required him to enter his social security number to gain access. That was the thing about talking to people at the IRS: A real paucity of secrets existed.

"Why do you want to know about White Rose, Samuel?" Lenore said when they were finally hooked back up.

"I've got a buddy, name of Eddie Champagne, who told me they were a great investment group," Sam said. He heard her clicking away in the background, and for a long time she didn't respond. It always bothered Sam that people in government had such poor phone skills, that they couldn't pretend to have chitchat while they sourced your every word. It was harder to do back when everyone was still working on typewriters, Sam wagered, though he was sure he would have been annoyed by the sound of the dinging return and papers being shuffled, too.

"Samuel, you know you're not investing anything. You need to see about getting more in your 401(k), you want my opinion," Lenore said finally.

"I was just going to give them a few thousand dollars," Sam said, not that he had a few thousand dollars. "My girlfriend, she's looking to put some seed into . . ." Sam didn't know what he was saying. He figured if he just let the words drift, Lenore would pick them up. She did.

"Let me put it to you this way," she said. "You give them money, you'll never see it again and, most likely, you'll be a plaintiff in about two months."

Lenore explained that White Rose was under investigation for mortgage fraud, but the problem was that no one had rolled on them yet. They were still making investors money, or at least enough to keep them hoping it was all legit. Right now, she said, it was the banks who were flagging them.

It was a classic scheme: White Rose used straw buyers to purchase land at full or slightly above full price; then they would bump up the price significantly on the contracts they sent to the mortgage lenders, thus generating huge extra fees on top of the mortgage. To make it all work, they had an accounting firm, two separate mortgage brokers and three different appraisers on the payroll. They had paperwork in order, she said, W-2s, pay stubs, everything, but it was all falsified. They ended up with the land, which they could resell, and which they usually did, flipping parcels within thirty days if they could, often for even larger profits based on the faulty appraisals, huge back-end fees and loans they'd have to touch. "They got people who got other people, too," Lenore said. "I wouldn't be surprised if they had a few flexible people at the banks, too."

"I guess I won't give them any money," Sam said, trying to sound as innocent as possible.

"Samuel," she said, "you can drop that ruse if you like. Our conversations are confidential."

"Are they really?" Sam said.

"Probably not," she said, "but if someone didn't want you getting this information, you wouldn't get it."

Sam knew that was one of the fringe issues related

to working with me—there were forces on the inside working for and against me. And if I was being tracked, Sam was being tracked, and all of this was getting approved by someone.

"How *not surprised* would you be about persons in the banks?" Sam asked.

"Enough to know that it's going to ring some bells on Wall Street," she said.

That sounded fairly dire. If Sam actually had stocks or bonds or whatever it was people did on Wall Street, he'd figure out how to utilize that information. He made a mental note to tell Veronica, since he was fairly certain she actually knew about that sort of thing.

"You got anything on their investors?" Sam said, figuring, *What the hell? Might as well just drop all pretense.*

Lenore told him it was just as simple as could be. People were being duped, but paid. Investors put in their money, were probably promised a healthy return, and then, at least to start with, got it. The market in Miami was hot, just like in every other metropolitan area with a halfway decent view. And just like every other place, the market had turned to shit. "It's just a matter of time before they stop getting dividends on investment," she said. "They've been running this now for quite some time without a hiccup."

It made sense to Sam, knowing that they were coming to Cricket every two weeks for cash. They were probably seeding their largest investors to keep the money flowing in, waiting for the next explosion in the market. But that hiccup? It was here.

"So Stanley Rosencrantz," Sam said. "Ballpark net worth?"

"Enough to fill a ballpark," Lenore said. "Won't matter, though, when he's doing Fed time."

Sam liked it when Lenore threw out terms like *Fed time*. This got Sam thinking. "Would it be possible to get a few of the addresses they've bought and sold?"

"No," Lenore said, but he heard her clicking in the background, and in a second his phone beeped, letting him know he'd received a text. That's how the IRS worked. They said no, but they meant yes. "Before I lose my job, is there anything else you might need to know, Samuel?"

He wasn't going to do it, but . . . "You have anything on Brenda Holcomb?"

Lenore gave out a perceptible sigh. He heard the familiar *click-clack* of keys again. "She's not right for you," Lenore said. "You be good and stay with Veronica."

"You're a sweetheart," Sam said. "But it's not like that."

"It's always like that with you, Samuel," Lenore said. He had to admit that she had a point. She'd been looking into women for him for too long. It was just his policy to make sure women he slept with weren't sleeper agents for terrorist organizations, or, at the very least, didn't have husbands in the mafia. "And, Samuel? You might want to tell your friend

Eddie Champagne, if you see him again, that he's now officially on the no-fly list, along with his friends at White Rose. In case you're curious."

"You caught that?"

"I catch everything," Lenore said. "Patriot Act, Samuel—you should learn to embrace it."

What Sam opted to embrace, after he hung up with Lenore, was the list of addresses she texted him. In the last year, there were three houses on Fisher Island, two office parks in North Miami, a dentist's office in Coconut Grove, a nightclub, a T-shirt shop, a strip club and an address Sam recognized immediately, since he'd spent the better part of the morning looking at it on Google Maps, trying to figure out how he was going to get his goddamned car back: the offices of Longstreet Security.

He had to hand it to Eddie Champagne. He was a scumbag, but man, he had huge balls.

Early the next morning, Sam recounted all of this to Fiona and me as we drove around Miami in Cricket's Mercedes (which I figured probably wasn't being monitored by any satellites—it at least didn't have any tracking devices on it), looking at the properties Eddie Champagne had purchased, flipped and lured investors into. We saw homes worth only a few hundred thousand dollars that he'd managed to get loans on for nearly a million dollars. We saw the remnants of the Lyric Theater in Overtown, one of the poorest neighborhoods in all of Miami, but which had once been the hub of what was called Little Broadway in

the thirties and forties, and which Eddie had managed to get a loan of four million dollars on, when
its value was more historical than nominal. And finally, we drove past Longstreet.

"The one building he actually still owns," Sam
said. "Or, rather, that White Rose owns. Longstreet
pays them a sizable amount of rent each month."

"Not a coincidence, I gather," I said.

"It wasn't even for sale when he bought it," Sam
said.

"How much did he pay for it?"

"Double its worth," Sam said.

"I admire his spite," Fiona said.

"Hard not to," Sam said.

I admired that he hadn't just done the easy job I
thought he'd done: What I'd figured from Barry's
description of Eddie's work and from what Stan had
said, was that it must be a low-impact, high-yield
operation. In truth, Eddie Champagne was just a few
steps away from being a legit businessman—the
steps being the ability to stay legit in a down-turning
market, a desire to do things legally, that sort of
thing. But like every other organized-crime syndicate
that operates in the real world, eventually, they
wanted to be taken seriously when they began to
make enough money to not want to risk death.

At least he wasn't another drug dealer dreaming
Tony Montana.

Dixon Woods, on the other hand . . .

We had other reasons to be at Longstreet, of
course, in that I expected the elusive Dixon Woods

would be coming in to mount up before meeting with his new best friend, Hank Fitch, and I wanted to be ahead of that, too.

Sam parked the Mercedes across the street from the facility in the lot of Clifton's Chips, a potato chip company, which, at only nine in the morning, was already like a hive of bees. There were men driving forklifts into and out of the warehouses with pallets filled with bags of chips. The parking lot was filled with Hondas and Toyotas and Saturns. There were already three women and one man—all wearing security badges and khaki on some part of their bodies, because security badges and khaki are like the uniforms for the depressed middle class— standing out front smoking around a trash can.

Two school buses pulled up then, and I watched as at least sixty children piled out and headed somberly to the front door. Nine o'clock is early for everybody.

"I always wondered how they got all of those chips in those lunch-sized sandwich bags without breaking any," Sam said, also watching the kids. "Now I get it. They have the kids put them in one by one. Ingenious."

"They're going on a tour," I said. I knew this because when I was a kid, I had done the exact same thing. I hadn't thought of it in years, and at the time the Clifton's Chips factory was in an older part of Doral, but I remembered walking through the factory and being transfixed by machines processing the chips, shooting them rapid fire onto conveyer belts, the women in hairnets plucking out burned chips one by one as they passed. I remembered how loud it all was, but how easy it was for me to concentrate in the noise, how some of the kids were crying and complaining of headaches, and I was just watching the machines, thinking about how they could be modified to spit fire instead of chips.

I also remembered that day because Nate got into a fight with a kid named Justin Pluck, and they had to shut down the whole facility because Justin stabbed Nate in the leg with a sharpened pencil, and Nate's blood got all over a batch of chips.

I also remembered that two weeks later, on Halloween night, Nate and I ambushed Justin Pluck and his friends with water balloons filled with Nair as they waited in the darkened parking lot at the evangelical church a few blocks from our house hoping to steal younger kids' candy. We spent all night searching, missing an entire night of candy gathering, just for the chance to get Justin.

It was worth it.

"That's the problem with education today," Sam was saying. "When I was a kid, we toured the armory. Generations of kids never get to see an armory anymore."

"I weep for them," Fiona said from the backseat. I couldn't tell if she was being sarcastic or if she was being serious.

After the children disappeared into the factory and the buses pulled away, I turned to Fiona, who had her laptop opened beside her. "Any word?" I asked.

"Nothing yet," she said. "At least not from anyone you're interested in. But I've heard from several men who sound very enticing."

I'd anticipated that, by now, Eddie Champagne would be trolling for a new woman on one of the widow sites, as Cricket called them, where Fiona now had her very own profile. I thought that my threat to Stan the day previous and the realization that Cricket's faucet had been turned off would get him scrambling. I figured that Fiona was bait he wouldn't be able to resist.

It wasn't for lack of trying on Fiona's part. She had posted several photos, including one that was just of her stomach, another that was just the curve of her right breast, another still that was just her lips, which, admittedly, were hard to resist. Half of the e-mails were from other women telling her she wasn't being tasteful. The other half were from men who didn't seem to have a problem and were offering airfare to pretty much every major American city.

"Jealous?" Fiona asked.

"Gratified," I said.

The fact was, everything was otherwise working well. I had Cricket's house set up for battle. I just had to get all the participants there, and things would take care of themselves. All that was broken would be fixed.

All I needed was for nothing to fall out of place, but already I was getting a bit of a moral tug. The money Stan was likely to get back to me was covered in the blood of others who'd been duped, too. The difference, I suppose, boiled down to choice. The investors who funneled their money to White Rose were guilty for being stupid, for being greedy, for not recognizing that what they were buying into couldn't be legit. Money can blind. It had, thus far, turned the investors mute, too. And soon it would all be moot. Maybe if it all closed down now, people would get some of their money back.

Maybe it was like Barry said. No one made a billion dollars by doing everything straight.

The money—or, rather, the appearance of it— would also help me out of my problem with Natalya. But Dixon Woods would have to cooperate to make that happen.

It was after ten o'clock before I realized that wasn't going to happen.

We were still parked across the street, watching the movements outside Longstreet. We saw Brenda Holcomb pull in for her day at work in a black Suburban. We saw another two dozen or so men drive onto the plant in their own Explorers and Expeditions, hop out in workout clothes and ten, fifteen minutes later come out dressed for work, which meant the same khaki pants the employees of the potato chip factory were wearing, except the Longstreet employees dressed the khaki up with navy blue sport coats and bulging necks. Office casual versus paramilitary couture. The men jumped into the company Hummers and sped off without even bothering to wave at the security guard, who, I noticed, was not the same man I'd dropped days before. Too bad. He was one of the only guys I'd gotten to do the vomiting trick.

After three Hummers left the lot, we could see that Sam's Caddie was right where it had been left. At least Bolts thought I was good for my word, even if she hadn't called me back. Before Sam could even comment, or begin complaining, five men came out of Longstreet in what looked to be black Armani suits accented by tight black T-shirts.

"Give me your binoculars," I said to Sam. He handed them to me, and I watched the five men stride across the lot. I only recognized one of them, but that was enough. Particularly since I also recognized that they were toting Hecklers to work, which seemed just slightly unusual.

I handed the binoculars to Fiona. "I wonder who their seller is," she said.

"Remind me and I'll ask," I said.

"Where do you suppose they're off to?" Fiona said.

"Salvation Army," Sam said. "The center cannot hold. They're our last defense against the forces of evil."

"Let me see your phone, Sam," I said. I showed Fiona the photo of the tacks on South Beach Sam took when he was in Bolts' office. "See the big guy in the middle?"

"They're all big," Fiona said.

"He was guarding Natalya when I met her at the hotel," I said.

"The Michael I first met wouldn't have let him keep walking," she said.

"It wasn't like we were in a bombed-out building in Beirut," I said. "I couldn't exactly shoot him in the knees while he stood in the lobby of the hotel."

"You should have shot him for wearing that shirt with an otherwise fine suit," she said. "I don't suppose this is all a coincidence."

"Bad people find bad people," I said.

"I can agree with that," Sam said.

"You don't actually believe Longstreet is an evil organization," Fiona said. "That's absurd."

"No," I said, "I don't think they are evil. I think they are in the business of making money. They don't have an institutional moral code or some kind of religious fanaticism to work against, so they just do what they do. I think they probably hire the kind of people who don't care how that money is made, provided they get their own cut."

"Say what you will about Bolts," Sam said, "but she was going to hook me up with a decent workers' comp package."

"All we know about Dixon Woods is rumor and innuendo," Fiona said.

"When did that ever bother you?" I asked.

"It doesn't," she said. "But I thought at least Sam would require a burden of proof."

"What I've been told is enough," Sam said. "Besides, a schmuck like Eddie Champagne knows you're a bad enough guy to use your name, that's like getting a notarized document from J. Edgar Hoover. Let's stick the fucker in Camp X-Ray and be done with it."

"We closed X-Ray in 2002," I said.

"Then let's bury him under it," Sam said, "whatever gets me my car back sooner."

Fiona's point about coincidence was well taken. But I knew I wasn't just seeing things.

With money came the need for security—that much I understood about Miami. In the case of Cricket O'Connor, her position in society, her affiliation with the war, and her ability to be manipulated by a person like Eddie Champagne opened the door to exploitation. That Eddie had taken on Dixon Woods' name was no coincidence—he held a grudge against a guy who'd beaten him, caught him at his game, and he harbored it enough to be creative with it, if for nefarious purposes.

That Longstreet was protecting Natalya was a coincidence in the barest sense: The Oro was owned by Russians with a pedigree for the drug trade. It was only natural that they'd hire private security for their *staff*, particularly those ex–KGB agents who probably would be wise not to find themselves in dangerous situations stateside, lest someone spike their sushi with polonium 210 when they got back home. And Longstreet, with their affiliations with the drug trade in Afghanistan, were probably happy to just take the check and not ask questions.

Dixon Woods was a fulcrum, even if he wasn't aware of it. My plan was to use that against him.

Then my phone rang. The number was blocked. At least I knew it wasn't my mother.

"Talk," I said. I'd spent some time thinking about

shortening my sentences to sound more menacing when the moment called for it. I figured it would make people mind the gaps in my speech; thought they'd think I was of so few words because my time was better spent planning on ways to kill them versus ruminating on tours of potato chip factories and Nair-filled Halloweens.

"It's Woods."

"Welcome to Miami," I said.

"We've got a problem," Woods said.

"We don't. You might. We don't."

"You don't seem to exist," Woods said. "I don't like to do business with people who don't exist."

"Hank Fitch doesn't exist," I said. "But his money does."

"You got any proof of that?"

I didn't. Not yet. I'd need Stanley Rosencrantz to come through. "This afternoon," I said. "My friend from the East is staying at the Hotel Oro. Are you familiar with that hotel?" Woods said nothing. I'd tried to play my hand too early, but now I had to keep bluffing. "We could meet there this evening, handle all of our business, and by morning you could be back on a plane for Afghanistan tending to your fields."

"It's off," he said and hung up.

I'd had conversations like that in the past. They were never good news.

"What was that?" Sam said. I told him. "Did it sound like he was in town?"

I thought about it. "Hard to tell," I said. "He

wasn't bouncing. There was no delay. Phone sounded like a cell. He could be in the PR for all that's worth."

"What now?"

"We make him show," I said.

I called Nate, whom we'd left at my mother's so he could watch over everything, in case any Communists showed up again, and to keep an eye on Cricket, who, for whatever reason, perhaps the same poor judgment that got her in this problem to start with, confided to Fiona that she felt safe around Nate whereas I scared her. "What time is it?" Nate asked when he finally answered his cell.

"It's after ten," I said. "Listen. Plans have changed. I need you to go to Cricket's and get the tear gas from the garage."

"I don't do business until noon," he said.

"It's already tomorrow in Australia," I said.

"So it's ten a.m. tomorrow," he said.

Nate's socialization process ended right around his sixteenth birthday. I had to constantly remind myself of this so that I didn't end up shooting him. "Nate," I said, "go to Cricket's. Now."

"Can I shower?"

"I don't know, Nate, can you?" Problem was, my socialization process as it related to dealing with Nate had stopped at around twelve. That was when we decided it would be easier to just fight over everything.

"Fine, fine," he said.

I gave him some specific instruction on how to

handle the tear gas. And upon reflection, told him to dig up the Malibu lights Sam had installed, too, which made Sam grunt with displeasure. I'd hear about that. But I thought we'd be able to use them in a more guerrilla-style soon. I should have known things were too perfect.

"You clear on everything?" I asked Nate. Asking Nate to do something came with a particular hazard: His involvement always made things worse. I was trying to learn to trust him, but I also knew that the definition of madness is repeating the same action over and over again and expecting a different result.

"How much am I getting for this job?" Nate asked.

"Nothing," I said.

"You have to be kidding," Nate said. "Cricket gets her money back, she could float us a couple Gs no problem. You want me to talk to her about that?"

"No," I said. "I just want you to do what I've asked."

"If there's some back end, I expect to be remunerated," Nate said.

"Consider that truck of suits your salary," I said.

"You're not nice," Nate said.

"Call me when you're back on the road," I said and hung up.

Next, I called Barry, who unlike Nate was awake and alert, if still Barry. "I need you to set up two bank accounts for me," I said. "But put them somewhere close. Nothing Swiss."

"How does the Dominican sound? I'm getting great rates there."

"Fine," I said. "I need one for Cricket O'Connor, one for Hank Fitch."

"Real ones or fake ones?" he said.

"Real for Cricket, fake for Hank," I said. I gave Barry Cricket's social security number, driver's license number, everything he might need.

"This Hank Fitch is a bad guy," Barry said.

"Yeah, I know," I said.

"He shot a guy I've done some business with in the past," Barry said.

"You don't say," I said.

"Heard things went down on the Fish," Barry said.

"Where'd you hear that, Barry?"

"Around," he said. "This might surprise you, but you aren't the only person who talks to me."

"Nothing surprises me," I said.

"People are moving money around on account of this Hank Fitch," he said. "Lots of it."

"Maybe the Fed is cutting the interest rate next week," I said. "How long to get this done?"

"Couple hours. What about that other favor? The loans? Or did that idea get shot up?"

"Funny," I said, again trying with the limited words thing. "I want you to set up an account for Eddie Champagne. See if you can fund a loan for him using this address as financial collateral," I gave him the address of Longstreet. I then gave him all the information contained on the police report Sam had finagled out of his guy at the FBI, which was enough to set up a legit account, except that Eddie Champagne's felony sheet would never allow him the loan without some fudging on Barry's part. "Run it through a real bank. Just keep yourself as out as possible. This is going to wake up some heat."

"Heat I can handle," Barry said.

"IRS heat," I said.

"Those guys are puppies," Barry said, but he actually had a touch of uneasiness in his voice. "Took them a decade to catch up to *Barry Bonds*. What do you think they'll do with me?"

"I appreciate it," I said.

Barry told me everything would be up within a few hours. "I'll text you all the numbers," he said, "but this phone is in the Atlantic. You need to find me, you know where to look."

"Keep whatever you can for yourself," I said.

"Implied," he said and was gone.

I had one more call to make. To Natalya.

"You think that's a good idea?" Sam said.

"It's not an idea," I said. "It's a trigger."

"You should just use a real one," Fiona said.

I dialed the hotel's general number, opting not to use the 800 number provided for me earlier. I told the operator I was calling from *Palm Life* magazine about doing a photo shoot at the hotel the following month and absolutely had to speak to the GM.

"This is Ms. Copeland," Natalya said, her accent perfect again.

"I have your money," I said.

"Smart," Natalya said. "Better for everyone that you come clean."

"Six o'clock," I said, "poolside at your lovely establishment. That way everyone goes home alive. I assume you have an account I can wire to?"

"Of course," she said.

"Good," I said. "And, Natalya, just so you know? I'm bringing my pit bull with me." I turned to see how Fiona took that.

Elated.

"What a nice reunion," Natalya said. "I haven't seen her since you and I slept together, Michael. At least not up close. We'll have much to discuss. Does she know about that spot under your left ear?"

"She knows them all," I said. "There's only going to be the two of us, so maybe call your friends at Longstreet and tell them they can leave their Hecklers at home for the night shift. We'll move the money and then I don't intend to ever see you again, correct?"

"It depends," Natalya said. "You seem to be doing well in business. Maybe you'd like to extend your reach?"

"Six o'clock," I said and hung up.

Now, all I'd need was the money, Dixon Woods and Eddie Champagne.

I looked at my watch. "Let's go," I said to Sam.

"What about Dixon?"

"He'll follow the money," I said. "That's what assholes do. Plus, he knows I took care of Eddie. Or at least that I told him I had." The truth was that I thought by the time I heard from Dixon that Eddie would no longer be a problem. "My guess? He's just taking some time to find out what Eddie has been doing. When he finds out he's been using Dixon's name, Eddie might stop being our problem entirely."

"Where to?"

I pulled out Stanley Rosencrantz's card and handed it to Sam. "Here." If I was going to get Cricket's money back, I was going to make sure I saw it happen.

12

If you decide to involve yourself in economic malfea-sance, even on a small level, you should pay atten-tion to the people you're doing business with. The odds are fair that if you've surrounded yourself with people willing to commit high-level subterfuge, there's a good chance they are actively planning their own exit strategies.

It would also be wise to think about keeping a low profile. Limit the number of business cards you print, and never give a spy your business card, even if you think the spy is a gun-toting maniac who shot one of your friends and beat the other down. This is par-ticularly true if you intend to actually go to your office and attempt to conduct business as usual when your friends are in the hospital.

White Rose's offices took up the fifteenth floor of a steel-and-glass thirty-three-story office building on Brickell Avenue, which means rents were high and

the kind of people coming in to do business with the
principals of the company very rarely carried guns.

"When you open your own security firm," Fiona
said as the three of us rode up in the elevator, "you
should definitely look into space in this building."

"I'd never have my own security firm," I said.

"Of course you wouldn't," Fiona said. "You'll be
the world's oldest spy. Ninety-nine years old and still
trying to figure out who burned you and why."

"Every day I'm closer to knowing," I said. If anything, what this Natalya situation informed me of
was that I was making headway in D.C., enough that
there were people fighting to keep me quiet without
too much involvement of their own. In the last year,
I'd seen so much, learned that every lead, even in
failure, provided something: Phillip Cowan, the man
who wrote up my dossier and filled it with lies? He
was just a clue, and he was already dead. And who
before him? Agent Jason Bly, who'd come to Miami
to silence me, and whom I eventually had to black-
mail, using my own bad reputation as the grist. And
of course the others: the assassins from my past,
alerted to my location and my lack of support; the
assassins from my present, sent to portray bureau-
crats like Perry Clark, who came to Miami to get me
off the books, just a signature was all he needed . . .
while he attempted to garrote me. What was he left
with? A gut shot, a nameless death.

And now Natalya. At least she came at me with
evidence first, probably out of unwarranted respect.

Maybe she didn't want to believe any more than I wanted to die.

"You and Sam can take on jobs finding lost dentures and libidos to fund your search. One day," Fiona said, "you watch."

"Day my pension comes through," Sam said, "I'm on a boat. Change in latitude. Change in attitude. Did you know, Mikey, that there is very affordable beachfront property in Nicaragua now? I'd have to keep my hat down in case any Sandinistas recognized me, but it would be a risk worth taking."

The elevator doors opened, and the three of us stepped out into the reception area of White Rose Partners. I still had my sunglasses on. Kept things mysterious.

As per usual, there was a receptionist sitting behind a desk prepared to greet us. As per usual, the receptionist was a young woman who looked like she'd be appearing on a reality show about a tanning salon with three of her wacky stripper friends before next Christmas.

In the last week, I'd dealt with more receptionists than in the previous ten years. Most terrorist organizations, warlords and assassination targets worked without receptionists, so I still didn't have the method of dealing with them down to a precise science, but I figured I'd give this one my best game. So when she asked if she could help me, I flashed her a grin as wide as the sea and said, "Could you tell Mr. Rosencrantz that the gentleman who shot his

friend Burl and permanently disfigured . . . uh . . ."
I couldn't remember the third fellow's name. I'd have
forgotten him entirely if I hadn't had to pull bits
of his tooth and bone from my skin using tweezers
that morning.

"Mr. White?" the receptionist said. Her expression
belied no fear. No comprehension, either.

"Danny?" I offered.

"Oh, yes," the receptionist said, eminently cheery.
"I know him as Daniel, but yes, same person."

"Great," I said. "So if you could tell Mr. Rosencrantz that the man who shot Burl and beat up
Danny is here to see him, that would be excellent."

"And your name, sir?"

"Hank Fitch," I said.

The receptionist picked up her phone. "Mr. Rosencrantz, I have Hank Fitch to see you. Okay. I'll tell
him." She hung up and smiled at us sweetly. "It will
be just one moment, if you'd like to take a seat."

"How do you do that?" Sam said once we were
sitting aside one another on a plush leather sofa.

"What?"

"That simple declarative bit where you say exactly
who you are, what you've done and who you'd like
to see. I mean, you told that girl you shot one of
her bosses."

"I smile a lot," I said. "The sunglasses help."

"He smells nice, too," Fiona said. She was flipping
through a brochure detailing precisely what White
Rose had to offer its clients.

"That helps?" Sam said.

"It's all sensory," I said. "Posture. A sense of confidence. That receptionist doesn't really think I shot her boss." To prove my point, I shouted across the lobby to the receptionist: "Any word on who shot your boss?"

"No, nothing yet," she said. "Can I get you coffee while you wait?"

"Beer?" Sam said. He tried with the smiling and the posture, which was met with a coy hair flip in return. "Perky girl."

Fiona handed me the brochure she was reading. "This sounds like a very enticing package," she said. In a glossy brochure featuring the stylized photos of *representative properties*, I learned that White Rose specialized in *preforeclosure* properties, which would mean, in essence, any property, and that they used funds derived from *equity partners* of which, if you were reading the brochure, you could now become one of. And what was promised? Securitized first mortgages. Interest above market rates. A full equity balloon payment and bonuses on resale of properties.

Basically? Horseshit.

Stanley Rosencrantz stepped into the lobby then and filled it with unbridled enthusiasm. "Hank," he said. "A pleasure. Won't you and your associates come into my office? I was just thinking I needed to contact you."

"Of course you were," I said.

After the next great plague, or after the ice caps melt and the world floods, or after the sun superheats our planet to 145 degrees in the shade, the only humans left standing to tend to the roaches, rats and flesh-eating zombies will be real estate agents. Stanley Rosencrantz might have his very own religious faction in his name by then.

The four of us—Stanley, Fiona, Sam and I—sat in a conference room together. Stanley had insisted on showing us his entire office, which seemed odd, until I realized he actually thought I just might be the kind of guy who wanted to come into an office every day, check on my criminal empire. Dixon Woods, I'm sure, never bothered to show up. Not if Eddie Champagne was smart.

Stanley made a great show of where Fiona and Sam could have their offices, too, though he had no idea who Fiona and Sam were and never bothered to ask, only referring to them as my associates. There were at least twenty-five people working in the office that morning—file clerks, secretaries, that sort of thing—who didn't look to have any idea what they were a part of. That Stanley, Burl and Danny did the collecting made sense, finally: keep the circle as closed as possible, only involving those who needed to be involved. Outsourcing muscle just to collect from Cricket would be expensive and unneeded—Eddie knew that. Best just to send his business partners.

We passed the offices for Burl and Danny as we walked—their names etched in glass on their doors—but Stanley didn't even mention them before finally opening up a conference room filled with bagels, coffee and juice, where we now sat.

"First thing," I said. "New rules." Stanley visibly

flinched, but didn't bolt. I felt like I owed him just a little reassurance. "Don't worry. I'm not going to shoot you."

I told Stanley that he was going to transfer five million dollars into Cricket O'Connor's account in the Dominican and gave him the account number Barry had texted me for the Banco Leon. "But before you start, here's the new rule, Stanley," I said. "I don't want that money coming from any of our investors' accounts."

"I'm sorry," Stanley said. "I'm not following you."

"How much liquid do we have here, Stanley?" I liked using *our* and *we* as each time it made Stanley wince.

"Liquid. Well. That depends on several factors."

"Just give the man a number," Fiona said. The thing about Fiona, she's done this sort of thing before, and not in the Robin Hood sort of way.

"Eight million dollars," Stanley said. "Maybe nine. Things have been difficult lately."

"Okay," I said. "And what about in your personal accounts. You, Burl, Danny, Dixon. How much do you four have?"

"Well, I don't have access . . ." Fiona reached into her purse and pulled out her gun, set it on the table. We hadn't really talked about this precisely, but that's what I loved about Fiona: She understood things as they were happening, adjusted on the fly, made things happen. "Another ten. Maybe twelve. Dixon kept his money elsewhere."

Of course he did. "Good," I said. "You transfer the five million dollars from your personal accounts."

"But that's money we've earned, Mr. Fitch," Stanley said.

"Really?" I said. "Is this a time to start arguing, Stan? Aren't I going to take care of *your* problems? Aren't I going to get rid of Dixon for you? That's not your investors' problem, now, is it?"

"The potential for a red flag to go up is . . . ," he started to say, but this time Sam, feeling emboldened by his conversation with Lenore no doubt put a hand up to stop him.

Sam put on his own sunglasses, which made his face look sort of round, put a stick of gum in his mouth and started snapping it with his tongue. Before it got to the level of performance art, Sam leaned across the table and extended a finger toward Stanley. "You want to know what a red flag looks like? I'm a red flag."

I had no idea what that meant, but Stanley seemed to know and that was enough. "Fine," he said. "Fine."

"And let's make it look right," I said. "I want you to set Cricket up as an investor in your company. What do you call them?"

"An equity partner," Stanley said.

"Right, an equity partner." When the Feds came sniffing, Cricket wouldn't be liable for anything. She'd have invested millions and taken at least a slight loss. Just like everyone else was about to. "And one last thing," I said. "I'm interested in getting started quickly out here, so I'd like a capital infusion of my own."

"How much?" Stanley said.

"Three," I said. I handed him Hank Fitch's Dominican account information, too. "And that you can cut from the investors, Stanley."

Forty minutes, several calls to bankers, all of whom seemed to be more than willing to do whatever Stanley asked, and which buttressed the claims Sam's IRS contact had, and two darkening rings of sweat under Stanley Rosencrantz' armpits later, it was done. Cricket O'Connor had five million dollars, legally. Hank Fitch had three million, illegally, but I didn't plan on keeping it. I just needed it for evidentiary purposes.

"Have you heard from Dixon?" Stanley asked casually after he printed out all of the appropriate documents.

"I haven't," I said.

"He said he was going to deal with you," Stanley said. He made a shooting motion with his hand. "Said something about you being in the wrong on the California deal, but that he'd settle it once and for all and that I had nothing to worry about. That after he got back from Afghanistan again, he'd deal with everything."

Afghanistan. Right. "He's wrong," I said. "About everything." Stanley nodded. He looked rather grave. He would look worse in a few months when he was doing federal time. "You have an address for Dixon?" I asked.

Stanley said he didn't, and for some reason, perhaps because there was no reason for him to lie, I believed him. "All I have is his cell," Stanley said, which I took. "You'll take care of him, right?"

"Didn't I say I would?" I said.

"Yes, Mr. Fitch. And in terms of Ms. O'Connor, I can presume she's still alive? That that issue has been cleared up to your satisfaction, and we can continue forward in our business dealings one to one with no fear of reprisal?"

"For now." This satisfied Stanley, as much as Stanley Rosencrantz could feel satisfied about anything, knowing, as I'm sure he did, that he was in with people way beyond his real estate training. "Do me a favor, Stanley," I said. "Send Burl and Danny fruit baskets in my name. Let them know there're no hard feelings, that I look forward to purchasing preforeclosure properties alongside them for many, many years. You can do that, right?"

Before Stanley could answer—and really, I don't know if he had a suitable answer, since he probably saw the course of his life and realized he'd need to cut and run as soon possible—we walked out of the conference room and left Stanley with what were probably his considerable thoughts.

"That went well," Sam said.

"Eight million dollars," Fiona said, "and you only shot one of them?"

"It's all posture," I said.

Ten minutes after we got back into the car, Nate called. "Were you expecting guests over at Cricket's?" he asked.

"No," I said. "What does the guest look like?"

"I can't see his face," Nate said. "He's wearing camo pants and a white T-shirt."

"Does he have a gun?"

"I can't tell if he's strapped or not."

"Do you?"

"I'm always packing," Nate said. I was afraid of that.

"Where are you?" I said.

"Upstairs. He just docked his boat. He's sort of pacing around, trying to act nonchalant. Taking a lot of time to tie it up. He just nodded at a woman walking her dog."

"What are you doing upstairs?"

"Cricket said she left some earrings up here that she wanted, so I thought I'd look for them."

I'd hold off on commenting on that until a later point. It would take us at least forty minutes to get out to Fisher Island, and that was if the ferry was just waiting for us to board. "We'll be right there. If you can," I said, "don't let him in, but don't let him leave if he gets in."

"On it," Nate said.

"Wait," I said. "Don't hang up." I told Fiona to call Eddie Champagne's phone, just to make sure that it wasn't the real Dixon Woods showing up to Cricket's, a situation that would be beyond Nate's limited scope.

"Ringing," Fiona said.

"Tell me what you see, Nate."

"Okay," Nate said. His voice turned official, which

made me sort of want to climb through the phone and shake the life out of him, but you take what you can get in these situations. "Perp is fishing in his pocket for something. Perp is pulling out a cellular phone device. Perp is looking at cellular phone device. Perp is hurling cellular phone device into the ocean."

Hello, Eddie.

"I'll be there," I said. "Don't do anything stupid."

"Why would I start?" he said.

Shit.

In a situation where it seems like the best course of action is to call the police and let them protect and serve, you should call the police. *Seems* is a nebulous emotion one should ignore. You should deal with certainty. You should know that if there is a man who has swindled a woman out of millions of dollars, a man who has swindled many others out of much more, you should be certain that that person needs to go to prison.

Unless, of course, you need to use that person as a pawn.

The facts were simple: We had Cricket's money back, but if I wanted to get out of my situation with Natalya, I needed Eddie Champagne. And I needed him alive or at least in reasonably decent shape. I needed him to have a paper trail.

I should have mentioned the reasonably decent-shape aspect to Nate. Because, after an hour of driving across Miami, waiting for the ferry and then finally making the slow crawl across the island back to Cricket's home, all without any word from Nate, I began to have concerns.

So when we walked into Cricket's house and found Nate and Eddie sitting at the kitchen table having a drink of Old Grand Dad, I must admit I was surprised.

That Eddie was bleeding from his head and had a package of frozen peas ACE bandaged around his neck, not so much.

"This is the guy I was telling you about," Nate said to Eddie when I walked into the kitchen. "We've been getting to know each other. I gotta say, Eddie has lived the life. He wrestled a polar bear once. Right, Eddie?"

"God's witness," Eddie said. He tried to raise his hands to give the Boy Scout salute, but I saw that Nate was smart enough to plastic flex cuff Eddie to his chair. Which explained the straw Eddie was using to drink with.

"Nate," I said. "A word?" I dragged Nate into the backyard and let Fi and Sam watch the drunken and beaten Eddie.

It was the afternoon and by all accounts another beautiful day in Miami, high in the eighties, a light breeze, blue sky, and my brother holding a bloody and beaten Eddie Champagne hostage in the kitchen of, in a way, his own home.

"You care to explain?" I said.

"I did as you said," Nate said, "except I amended the plan."

"Yeah, I see that."

Nate said that when he got off the phone with me, he started thinking about how awful he felt for Cricket, and for all the other people he was sure Eddie had rooked, and just couldn't control his emotions any longer. So he walked downstairs, unlocked the front door and, when Eddie came though a few minutes later, hit him in the back of the head with his gun.

"But then he started gushing blood," Nate said, "just prodigious amounts, and it was all matted with hair, and I thought, Oh, no, I don't want a stiff on my hands. So I tried to dress his wound the best I could."

First perp. Now stiff. I didn't know if I'd be able to handle Nate in his new crime-fighting mode for much longer. "Frozen peas?" I said.

"The freezer was all out of ice," he said. "And then he came to and was really complaining about the pain, crying, moaning, the whole experience, so I figured, you know, a swab of old Old Grand Dad on the wound would dull the sensations and keep out infection, like in those Westerns Dad used to watch."

"That was TV," I said. "You ever hear of Bactine?"

"Yeah," Nate said, "that thought came to mind after the whiskey really got poor Eddie jumping, so I figured, give the guy a couple sips, see if that made a difference."

"Poor Eddie?"

"The guy has had some tough breaks," Nate said.

"I'm sure," I said.

"Anyway," Nate said, "we got to talking. Comparing notes. He's really done well for himself in this real estate game."

"He's a crook, Nate," I said.

"If you can look past that," he said.

"I can't," I said. "Neither should you. He tried to bleed Cricket dry. God knows how many people just like her didn't get out. The guy is a predator, Nate. Do you get that?"

"Okay," Nate said. "Okay. Breathe, man. You're all bunched up looking now. Your eyes are all buggy. Big mean spy guy going loco."

I unclenched my jaw. I loosened up my forehead. I took a moment to stare at the sea. I thought I caught a whiff of someone grilling chicken.

Nothing worked.

"Nate," I said, "did he tell you what he was doing here?"

"He said he was worried about his wife," Nate said.

"I'm sure," I said.

"Yeah, I didn't believe that, either," Nate said. "So I asked him again after we'd had a couple. But that's the story he's sticking to. Said he figured if some crazy psycho was willing to kill her in the name of someone he was just pretending to be, that he owed it to her to set the record straight."

"A real come-to-Jesus moment," I said. "You did good, Nate. I appreciate it." I meant it, even if Nate's methods were a wee bit on the unorthodox side.

"Yeah?" Nate said.

"Yeah."

"Just keeping my pimp hand strong," Nate said. I started to walk back inside, since I had an idea how I'd use this situation with Eddie to the fullest, but Nate stopped me. "Do you remember coming out here when we were kids?" I told him I did. "What was it, some kind of field trip or something?"

"Yeah," I said. "Something like that."

"I remember you and me just running around that big-ass resort," he said. "And then I sort of remember us hanging out with a security guard. Weird. I haven't thought about that in years."

"It was a good time," I said. I didn't have the heart to tell him what I remembered, the circumstances, the repercussions.

"Was it?" he asked. He turned his head, as if trying to get his memories to line up.

"Sure, Nate," I said. "Sure. Not like when we went to that potato chip factory and Justin Pluck stabbed you."

"You know I ran into Justin Pluck a few years ago," Nate said. "Married, a couple rug rats, working at Costco."

"Was he still missing most of his hair?"

Nate laughed. "I didn't get too close. I didn't want whatever he had rubbing off on me."

"What did he have?"

"Normalcy," Nate said.

That was something he—we—would never have.

After sending Nate home, I went inside, brewed a carafe of coffee, sat down with Fiona and Sam in front of Eddie Champagne and started pouring him cups of black coffee.

"Drink," I said to Eddie.

"That's a myth," he said. "Coffee doesn't sober you up. Best thing for me would be a nice, long nap. Clinically proven."

"I'm sure it is," I said. I nodded at Sam, who reached over and squeezed Eddie's nose closed for about ten seconds, until Eddie popped open his mouth to breathe and Fiona shoved a straw in. "Now be a good boy, Eddie. Drink."

Eddie did as he was told, downing two cups of coffee in record time. I made him a couple pieces of toast and made him eat those, too. When he started to show signs of actually being able to comprehend reality, I let Sam take a look at the gash on the back of his head, which was still leaking blood, but not quite the torrent Nate had mentioned.

"He'll need stitches," Sam said.

"How many?" Eddie said.

"I'd say about fifty," Sam said.

"That's about two hundred less than you would have required if it had been me here," I said. "About a thousand less than you'll need if you don't tell me what I want to know now."

"First thing you need to know," Eddie said, "I am

not the guy you're mad at. Dixon Woods? That's just a name I picked at random. This is a big misunderstanding."

"I know who you are," I said. "And I know you just lied to me. I'm not the police, Eddie. You're not on tape. We're just two guys having a conversation. Granted, one of us is cuffed and one of us isn't, but I'd like you to feel like you can tell me the truth, Eddie. I gave you coffee. I made you some toast. So I'm going to give you a chance to correct that last statement. If I like what you have to say, I won't spray salt water into your head wound."

Eddie Champagne's eyes darted around the room. He didn't look scared. He didn't even look worried, exactly. He sort of seemed to be enjoying this.

"You know," he said, "we redid this kitchen."

"I didn't know that," I said.

"Yeah," he said. "I moved in, it was stainless steel. Real cold, uninviting. It was my idea to put in those glass-faced cabinets. I picked out the granite for the island, made Cricket get one we could put chairs around. She wanted to have a sink in the island, but I told her she wouldn't need it since she wouldn't be doing that much cooking. She liked that idea. Let me tell you. What lady wants to cook?"

He looked at Fiona then and gave her a crooked smile, which probably gave other women a warm feeling, but which only caused Fiona to glare at him. That had a silencing effect on Eddie.

"When did you decide to bleed her?" I said.

"You don't just decide that sort of thing," Eddie said.

"More of a life choice?" Sam said.

Eddie cleared his throat. "I've got a few abilities," Eddie said, "none of which make for a good living. But after I met Cricket, I really thought she was the kind of lady I could get used to loving. But then, once I got in it, all these lies I'd already told, what was I supposed to do?"

"Telling the truth would have been an angle," I said.

"Not gutting her life," Fiona said.

"Not stealing money from wounded soldiers," Sam said.

"So there are three choices," I said. "You want more?"

Eddie pointed to his coffee cup, indicated he'd like some more. In a show of good faith, I clipped off Eddie's cuffs, told him that if he did anything outwardly stupid with his hands he'd lose the use of them, permanently. I poured him another cup and watched him take a few sips. He held his pinky out at an angle, like he was of the royal class. He had all the moves.

"Guys like you and me, Hank, we can't always deal in truth. Look at you and your crew here," he said. "I don't presume to know what your game is, but I'm going to say you've never met Dixon Woods, either, or else you wouldn't be trying to play that psycho. That pussy Rosencrantz just swallowed your whole bait. Teach me to work with educated people. Am I right?''

Smart. Trying to make a connection with me. Attempting to get an empathetic response. Probably thinking, like Stanley Rosencrantz before him, *Here's a guy I could make a deal with.*

"Eddie," I said, "we're nothing alike."

"Don't be so sure," he said. "I mean, here you are with Cricket, too. Similar tastes, right? And anyway, I came back today. I was ready to take you out. See? End of the day, I felt bad. Contrite. Ready to make amends."

"Yeah," I said. "Listen. I hate to tell you this, but I do know Dixon Woods. And I'm afraid, Eddie, that you're going to need to deal with him yourself."

Eddie finally seemed to leave his comfort zone. "That guy is a monster. You can't let him have his way with me." Eddie detailed his last meeting with Dixon, which involved a tire iron, a broken wrist and a lingering jaw problem. "I want it noted for the record," he said, leaning into his coffee cup, like it was microphone, "that I really did love his mother. You know, she passed on and that bastard didn't even have the kindness to come back for her funeral. No problem busting me up, but he won't do the honor of burying his mother? You look up the records, see who paid for her funeral expenses. Tell your people *that*."

"Noted," Fiona said.

Eddie started to say something, but then stopped, looked hard at Fiona. "Do you do any modeling?"

"No," Fiona said, though I could see where this was headed.

"You look familiar. Your lips, for some reason. And no disrespect, but your right breast, too."

"I have very uncommon breasts," she said.

"You ever do any calendar work?" Eddie asked. "Maybe I saw you online somewhere?"

"I'm in a coed naked volleyball league," she said.

Eddie again tried to say something, but it didn't seem like his mouth was working, which was good, because I was done talking to him, his very voice making me sick. "Sam," I said, "cuff and gag him."

"What?" Eddie said. "I thought we were getting along."

"Yeah," I said, "you thought wrong."

After we got Eddie subdued again, we sat him in the living room, which frankly smelled awful and would require an industrial cleaning very soon, and I snapped a few photos of him. When we had one that looked sufficiently morbid, I put in a call to Brenda Holcomb at Longstreet. Sam told me to make it a point not to call her Bolts. "She finds it disrespectful," he said.

"Brenda," I said when she answered "this is Hank Fitch. The man who didn't kill you."

"You've caused a lot of problems, Hank."

"I know," I said. "I'm sorry about that. But I'm calling you now to do you a favor, show I'm good on my word."

"I already called Dixon," she said. "What he does, he does."

"Right," I said, "I get that. But listen. I have a guy here whose been impersonating Dixon for the last two years. He's made Dixon a lot of enemies. But he's also made Dixon a lot of money."

Silence. Money always causes silence.

"You still there?" I asked.

"Go on," she said.

"I have a picture of him I'd like to send to you, that if you could forward it on to Dixon, I think we could end all of our mutual problems." *Hopefully by around six,* I thought. "Do you have a number I can use?"

Brenda sighed. "I lose my job, I come after you."

"You wouldn't want to do that," I said.

"Who are you, exactly? Because you're not Hank Fitch."

"I am today."

"The only Hank Fitch I could find in all of America is married to a woman named Linda and lives in Utah with his eight kids. You don't sound like the marrying kind. Or the Mormon kind."

"You'd be surprised." Brenda gave me a number and I sent the photo to her. "One other thing. My friend's car. Good faith."

"You two run a clean operation. I couldn't find a thing of use in that car," she said.

"Why don't you park it across the street, and we'll call it all even?"

"You have a strange idea of even, Mr. Fitch," she

said, but then agreed, though she sounded more resigned than anything.

"Did the pictures come through?" I asked.

Silence.

"Yes," a male voice said. I guess all that silence
was Brenda patching me in to Dixon. "Where is he?"

"Right now? He's sitting across from me. Where
he'll be is wherever you want him to be if it means
we deal. I need that product."

"Put him down," Dixon said. "Send me a photo
when you're done."

"I'm not going to kill him," I said. Eddie actually
sighed through his gag, which isn't something you
hear very often: a person sighing with relief while
bound and gagged. "I'm happy to let you." Eddie's
joy? Short-lived. "I hope you can understand."

"Where's your money?" he asked.

"The Dominican," I said.

"Give me the digits," he said.

Just like Sam, just like me before all of this, Dixon
had contacts. If he wanted to know how much
money was in a secure account, I have every belief
he'd be able to find out, so I gave him the account
number.

"Hold on," he said. A few moments later, Dixon was
back. His entire disposition was changed. "Where'd
you want to meet?"

"Hotel Oro," I said. "That work for you?"

"Yeah," he said. "Nice place. That's the one with
cabanas, right?"

"Right."

"Why don't you bring me one of Champagne's fingers as a gratuity?"

"I'll bring you something better. Eddie and his bank account information so you don't need to beat it out of him. He's been very busy on your behalf. Six fifteen?"

"I'll be there," Dixon said and was gone.

I looked at my watch. It was three o'clock now. We didn't have much time, but I was going to make this work. In order to do that, I'd need to get Eddie to calm down—since he was now apoplectic—and I'd need to get the Hotel Oro ready to my specifications.

"Sam," I said, "I'm going to need you to do me a favor."

"Whatever, Mikey," Sam said.

"I need you to blow up the Hotel Oro," I said.

13

When you're a spy, certain things are much harder than you'd think. You begin to expect that the entire world thinks like you do and therefore has an implicit understanding that actions have consequences. You start thinking that people will look at the world and will realize that it's better to just be good, that it's better not to pull every dog's tail, that it's better to live your life, earn your money, live within your means and if sometimes a deal falls into your lap that seems too good to be true, it's because it is and you should run like hell.

So if you're not a spy, you should pay your parking tickets. You shouldn't own a TEC-9, much less try to deduct one from your taxes, and you shouldn't have sex with people you'd have no compunction killing.

You shouldn't, finally, pretend to be someone you're not—because, eventually, you'll end up like Eddie Champagne, with a guy like Dixon Woods on

your ass and the rest of the world coming to pieces
around you, including a former Navy SEAL named
Sam Axe using you to help him place small bombs
inside a luxury hotel in Miami.

Sam didn't want to do it, but I told him it was the
best way to dispose of Eddie Champagne without
actually getting Eddie Champagne disposed, so the
two of them left Cricket O'Connor's house and
headed to the Hotel Oro, where he'd reserved a room
under Eddie's name and even used Eddie's credit
card. Making a paper trail.

The way Sam had it figured, being placed in
charge of Eddie Champagne wasn't the worst job in
the world, especially since he sort of liked the elegance of triangulation. It was just the checking-in that
concerned him, since he'd need to convince Eddie to
be equally elegant while being forced into a posh
hotel against his will.

And in plastic cuffs.

We all knew that if Eddie bolted, we might never
see him again, and that just wouldn't work. You rack
up a bill, you pay your debt.

So after parking Cricket's Benz across the street in
self-parking, figuring maybe waiting for the valet at
the end of the evening wouldn't be the best bet, all
things considered, Sam broke it down for Eddie.
Eddie was still half sauced, though with all that coffee, toast, fear and anxiety he'd found a sort of
stoned equilibrium and had actually broken down in
tears in the car while Sam drove, realizing that they
were literally driving in *his* car. Sam couldn't figure

out if the tears were real or another ploy, but they helped him with the plan.

"Here's the deal, Ed," Sam said. "I'm getting real tired of how Hank is running our crew." Co-opting Eddie's language was sort of fun for Sam, though he thought that Eddie had probably picked up his vernacular from someone else, too. "You and me, we sort of see eye to eye on a lot of things."

Eddie wiped his nose on his shoulder. "Yeah?"

"Yeah," Sam said. "Way I figure it, you and me? We could work together down the line. Who knows?" Sam saw the rotors working in Eddie's head already.

"Absolutely," Eddie said.

Absolutely, Sam thought. The thing about most criminals is that they aren't wicked—they're stupid. They're opportunists. "I'm going to try to get this Dixon problem away from you in a way that doesn't, you know, end up in your death."

"Thanks, buddy," Eddie said. He sounded like he really meant it, which he probably did.

"But you're going to have to man up some," Sam said. *Man up*. Who talked liked that? "Take a broken arm. Maybe another broken jaw. Or maybe just a bullet somewhere fatty." Sam gave him a poke in the shoulder, which, Sam was disturbed to find, was about as fatty as his own shoulder. He really needed to start cutting out starches.

"I've had worse," Eddie said. He was actually getting jubilant.

"Okay," Sam said. "But you need to cooperate

with me. No scene in the hotel at check-in. No shitting yourself or anything nasty."

"Done," Eddie said.

"We get to the room, you cooperate, and you have my word, you will see tomorrow."

"Maybe you'll take me to see Cricket? I mean, of course, if everything ends up kosher?" Sam saw that Eddie had tears in his eyes again. Incredible. The guy was either in line for an Oscar, or he was really starting to feel the weight of his deceptions.

Sam put his money on the Oscar. "Sure, Eddie, sure."

Eddie pursed his lips in thought again. "You think, maybe, I could get some room service, too? Maybe a steak?"

Oh, yeah, Sam thought, *the Oscar is his.* But that was okay. If it was enough to get him into the hotel and maybe get him to trust Sam a bit, he was willing to get the man a steak for his troubles. "We'll get two," Sam said, and then he pulled Eddie out of the car, put a coat over Eddie's cuffed wrists, grabbed a duffel bag out of the trunk—a duffel bag filled with solar Malibu lights and some light soldering equipment—and made his way into the hotel.

True to his word, and much to Sam's surprise, Eddie was the perfect prisoner at check-in, so much so that Sam went ahead and placed his room service order right there at the front desk. Even threw on an extra 50 percent tip ahead of time. It was Eddie's bill, after all.

And after they finished their steaks—Sam had the

T-bone; Eddie opted for the filet; both had the hot butter—Sam had to admit that Nate had been right. The guy could talk. He didn't mention to Sam wrestling a polar bear, but he did have a story about a bison. They got to having such a great time, Eddie didn't even mind when Sam asked him to hold on to the devices he was building, his greasy fingerprints leaving smudges of himself on everything—the inside parts, the outside parts, the triggers, the soldered pieces, everything.

Sam couldn't figure out if Eddie knew what he was doing or not. Maybe he had just decided prison would be better than Dixon Woods in a locked room.

The sap.

Either way, it didn't matter to Sam. He'd be long gone by the time Eddie Champagne figured out that decision definitively.

Sam stepped out onto the secluded balcony overlooking the Hotel Oro's pool and set up his homework project. When he was through, he made two calls: one to the IRS and one to the FBI.

Just before six, Fiona and I pulled up at the Hotel Victor, the hotel directly next to the Hotel Oro, and parked in one of the spots directly out front reserved for people checking in. The sign said thirty minutes only, which was about ten minutes longer than I thought it would take us to do our job.

Outside it was one of those nights when Miami feels laced with magic: A mist of fog was in the air, so the glittering lights of South Beach cast a glow into the world, giving the impression you were already remembering what you were experiencing, a soft focus with, at different angles, a sharp glare of truth, of reality, that you were alive in a moment.

I wore a light tan-colored suit, a collared shirt open at the neck, a red pocket square that I removed when I saw that Fiona was wearing a short red dress that would have made Audrey Hepburn give up cocktail numbers for good. We didn't want to match, look too much like tourists after all, particularly since if we weren't careful, our pictures would be in the paper.

Or *Palm Life*, since an hour earlier Jay Gatz had given James Dimon a call. "James, sport," I said, "I thought you'd be interested in an ad hoc event taking place this evening at the Hotel Oro. Daisy thought you might appreciate the visual experience."

"Mos def," he said.

I almost hung up, thought it wasn't worth the two minutes of my life I'd lose to hear James Dimon speak one more word, but marched on nonetheless. The greater good and all that. "Come at six fifteen," I said. "There's a fantastic new Russian model named Natalya Choplyn we'll be entertaining poolside. She's very underground overseas but is about to"—I paused for just a moment, in case I couldn't control the bile in my throat—"jump off here. This would be a real get for you."

"Hot," he said.

"Very," I said. "Let me spell that last name for

you. C-H-O-P-L-Y-N. Make sure you get that down."

Now, sitting with Fiona in the Charger, I couldn't help but wonder what would become of Natalya after this evening. I had a sense that she'd find herself intimately acquainted with the laws governing economic espionage, particularly economic espionage committed by a foreign national on American soil. Fifteen years would be a good starting point if Natalya wasn't ex-KGB, but since she was, there was a good chance the government—ours or hers—might just disappear her after they—the IRS, the FBI, Putin himself—became aware of the transfer of millions of dollars into her account, particularly millions of dollars derived from bogus mortgages.

And if I could time it just right, she'd be sitting with Dixon Woods when it happened.

"You ready?" I said to Fiona.

"Remind me again why I don't get to shoot Natalya?"

"Public place, bigger fish to filet," I said. "We can get in and out and not even wrinkle our clothes."

We stepped out of the car and made our way across the street, sidestepping spillover lines of people from clubs on either side of the street. The people outside had their own unique blush this evening, but then everything felt different to me the moment before action.

Everything slows.

Colors become brighter.

It's as if I can see all the moves before they even happen.

A few steps before the Oro's front door, I stopped Fiona, who was walking with a rather purposeful gait. "You ready?"

"Let me check my purse," she said. She was holding a red Kate Spade bag under one arm. "Five vials of tear gas, a Sig, a BlackBerry, some lipstick. I'm set for the evening. No condoms, though, so let me know if we need to stop off."

I looked up at the length of the Hotel Oro. Sam was in room 511, overlooking the pool. He and Eddie Champagne were just another couple having a good time, for all the staff of the hotel knew. At six, just to let us know he was in his room, he would flash the room lights five times, followed by another eleven times, so I'd know for certain the game was afoot.

At this point, at this hotel, with whoever was watching, things had to be as low-tech as possible. In a confined space like a hotel, picking up cell signals, if you're looking for a specific one, is freshman-year-at-Quantico sort of stuff.

A moment later, the flashing started. Sam was in. We were about to be.

We had thirty minutes to make it happen.

We strode past the valet station and I gave a cursory glance for my favorite bookie/valet but didn't see him, though it was hard to be sure who I was seeing, since they were all wearing that same black suit.

"Black Armani is out," Fiona said.

"You get that?"

Once into the lobby, it was Miami bass and Miami style—the bronzed bodies happy to laze in the cabanas on my previous visit were now thumping across the two bars, filling the dance floor, the cabanas moving right along with them. Lining the walls, looking appropriate surly, were Longstreet men, sweating through their black T-shirts and suits, their entire paramilitary careers boiled into watching other people have a good time. From backing up strike forces to backing that ass up.

We all make choices.

As we walked, the crowd moved imperceptibly away from us. Neither Fi or I projected much of a good-time vibe, and that was good. If they got too close to Fi, she was liable to crack tear gas on the floor just to see the expression on their faces.

We passed the serpentine reservation desk, and I looked for Star but didn't find her, either. Forever must have come to a close. Or maybe she got that job modeling at Abercrombie. Or maybe Natalya had her killed for knowing my name. All were possibilities, none that I could ruminate on now, the music pounding in my ears, adrenaline pushing me out the door to the pool area, where the people nearly having sex at the bar looked positively Amish by comparison.

The infinity pool worked alive with movement, men and women writhing to the same nameless beat from inside, huge amps spreading the dusty bass into the air. Servers whose only bit of indulgence was a strip of fabric over their nipples moved through the crowded tables, stopping every few steps to drop off drinks, pick up glasses, and bend over suggestively in front of men and women wearing even less clothing.

"It smells like sex out here," Fiona said. "We should stay. Get a room."

"I don't think that's a good idea."

"Maybe we'll come back for lunch one day. Your mother never did get to eat that day, Michael."

I spotted Natalya the moment we entered the pool area. She sat at a round table just adjacent to the rear bar, a nice crowded locale, but with a fine exit as well, since the bar backed up against the low shrubbery separating the hotel from the ocean. It wasn't beyond reason to assume there was a boat out there, waiting. But it was impossible to see, since the beach was covered with people, some just gawking at the crowd inside the Oro, others simply sitting in the cooling sand, watching the water.

Natalya was alone at the table, but I counted three Longstreet men on a first-floor balcony—smart—and three men who looked like, well, Communists, with their pale skin and inability to find a beat, trying to look natural at the far end of the bar. They were wearing shorts and white T-shirts, their sunburns practically glowing through the fabric.

"In and out," I said to Fiona. We were only steps away.

"My pleasure," she said.

I looked up into the sky. I didn't see any large spy satellites, so that was nice. But I did see Sam, right where I knew he would be. Or, rather, I saw the light inside Sam's room.

Natalya stood up when she saw us. "Michael," she said, professional charm oozing from her, "it's such a pleasure." She leaned toward me and gave me an air kiss on either cheek. Putting on a show.

"Hello, Ms. Copeland," I said, figuring, *You want a show? We'll give you a show.*

She turned to Fiona and tried to give her the same air kisses. "Touch me," Fiona said, "and you'll be eating out of a feeding tube. Respectfully." Fiona wasn't much for shows.

"By all means, have a seat then," Natalya said.

"Yes, I have opium to buy and sell to little kids," I said, as we sat down. "Wish I had more time to chat. But I'm sure you understand."

Natalya frowned. Visibly frowned. "I thought once we were done here, the three of us could be sociable. All in the game, isn't it? It's not me you're mad at, Michael. In the same situation, you would have done the same thing."

"There wouldn't be a same situation," I said. "I would have killed you. Money means nothing to me."

Natalya picked up a glass of water from the table and took a sip. There were two other glasses and a pitcher, but I'd already told Fiona that Natalya liked her poisons.

"Apparently," Natalya said.

"And this isn't a game," I said. "You threatened my life. Fiona's. My family's. So you'll excuse the lack of my desire on our part to let bygones be bygones. Save 'Auld Lang Syne' for New Year's and all that. Plus, I count six guys ready to shoot me."

"Perceptive," Natalya said.

"Realistic," I said.

Fiona reached into her purse to pull out her Black-Berry, and all six men moved forward, which caused Fiona to stop midreach. "Care to tell *your* pit bulls to sit and stay?" Fiona said.

Natalya gave both groups of men a nod, and they shrank back to more relaxed positions. It took her a few moments, but Fiona eventually accessed Hank Fitch's Dominican account. "Where to?" she asked.

"If you don't mind?" Natalya said, indicating the BlackBerry. "I just want to make sure what you say is happening is happening."

"Be my guest," Fiona said and handed her the BlackBerry. Natalya looked over the information, which was mostly just several zeros and a three. It was all legitimately in the account—of course, Hank Fitch didn't really exist, his account consisting of falsified documents on every turn—and the money certainly existed. It had been transferred from the accounts of White Rose Partners—in a legal, traceable transfer, though one that was certainly being monitored now by all sorts of agencies—into Hank Fitch's account, and it would now be transferred, legally, into an account held by Natalya. Of course, she'd be smart enough to have a shell set up somewhere, but that wouldn't matter.

"You've done nice work, Michael," Fiona said.

"I get good rates in the Dominican," I said. "You should consider keeping your money there."

"I've always preferred Nicaragua," she said and handed Fiona a slip of paper with her account information.

"Wait," I said to Fiona. "Tell me one thing, Natalya. Out of courtesy for the game. Who is your source?"

Natalya leaned back in her chair and exhaled. "You know I can't tell you that, Michael. He'd stop being my source."

"Three million dollars doesn't buy you what it used to," I said.

"The American dollar is weak," she said, but there was something eating at her. "I can tell you this. You're doing yourself no favors in this drug business. Get yourself a job. Get away from whatever answers you need to be searching out. Because my source has been in your government for a long time, Michael. Longer than both of us. And he says you're as culpable in that weak American dollar as anyone."

"I haven't done what my dossier says," I said. "So you tell Yuri that the Cold War is over. Tell him to cash his checks and come back to the Motherland. Tell him . . ." A flashing light caught the corner of my eye.

Sam telling me it was now, which meant Dixon

Woods was in the building. A little early. Not surprising.

"Just tell him," I said.

"I'll do that," Natalya said, but I saw her looking over my shoulder. She must have caught the light, too, though she didn't seem alarmed. Must have thought it was just a light, nothing more.

"Are we done rattling sabers, Michael?" Fiona asked.

"Go ahead," I said.

In just a few keystrokes, three million dollars passed from the account of Hank Fitch into the account of Natalya Choplyn. We waited silently for the confirmation from both banks, and when it came, I heard Natalya give out a thick sigh. She turned and waved away the men behind her from Longstreet, who shrugged and went inside their room. Three guns down.

She then looked at the three men at the bar and nodded once. There was a grave look on her face, one I hadn't seen before, and I realized that those men weren't guarding her—they were watching her, making sure that she did what she was supposed to do, that the scales were evened. Natalya Choplyn's life was saved, though not for long.

"They have your kids?" I asked.

"No," Natalya said. "No. Of course not. It's not like that anymore, Michael."

"It isn't?" I said.

Natalya didn't answer.

"You don't even have children, do you?" Fiona said.

"We should celebrate," Natalya said.

"That's the laugh, Michael," Fiona said. "I think she fooled you. I can tell she's married, certainly, that round of fat around her chin. It's disgusting, really, letting yourself go like that, Natalya. But she's not stupid enough to actually procreate."

"You know nothing," Natalya said.

Sam hit the lights again.

"Your lookout is trying to get your attention," Natalya said. "You'd better give him the okay sign. I'd hate for someone to get shot now that the deal is done."

Shit.

I turned and waved at Sam, though I couldn't see him. I looked at my watch. We had about five minutes to get out of this situation, which was good since I saw Dixon Woods striding through the crowd.

He was a big man—over six three—and he looked the part he was born to play: He fairly screamed Special Forces with his square head and closely cropped hair, a jaw line that was dashed with hints of stubble, arms that grew larger on the outside of his short-sleeved shirt. When I saw him in real life, the comedy of Eddie Champagne was clear. Where Dixon Woods was all coiled muscle, Eddie was doughy and simple. The sharpness of his cons certainly didn't translate to his body, but then a woman like Cricket would probably never know the difference, and men like Stanley Rosencrantz and his partners only cared about the stories he could tell and the myth that exists in secrecy.

Even from our table, I could tell Dixon Woods was the real deal.

"You're right," I said to Natalya. "We should celebrate. It's just a game, isn't it? And here we are, three survivors. Let me get the first round."

I got up before Natalya could say a word and walked directly toward Dixon, my eyes steady on his. There was a look of recognition on his face.

"Woods," I said when I was near him. I'd make this quick.

"Westen?" he replied.

Shit again.

"Yes," I said. I tossed my head from side to side. "You have to pardon me. I am *drunk*!"

"Belgrade, right?"

"I wasn't there," I said.

"Neither was I," he said.

I pointed at him. He pointed at me. It was like we were in a very bad boy band and about to do a dance number. I grabbed him by the shoulders and gave him a big man hug. He had a gun on his back, probably a nine. I nudged his leg with mine and felt something solid on his ankle, probably a knife.

"What are you doing here?" I said far too loudly, all joy and conviviality.

"Business." He looked around. Not nervously. Just checking the scene. "Let me ask you: You ever hear of a guy named Hank Fitch? I'm supposed to meet him here."

"That kind of business," I said. I shook my head. "I try to keep my nose straight, know what I'm saying?"

"I hear you," he said. "Bills, man. You know how that goes. I'm working private now."

"Where've you been?"

"Fighting Jihads, making money," he said. Just two old friends we were. Now he was sizing me up. "You were a bad man."

"Weren't we all," I said. I pointed at the table where Fiona and Natalya were still sitting. That they hadn't come to blows yet was nothing short of a miracle. "Why don't you join us for a drink?"

Dixon looked around. Thought about it. "I'm meeting that guy," he said. "Fitch."

"One drink," I said. "Won't kill you, right?"

"I haven't been back in Miami in a long time," he said, feeling the vibe now himself, acting like people do when they wish they were drunk. "A drink won't kill me. You—you I'm not so sure about."

"Belgrade," I said, like we had been in a fraternity together, and I was remembering the Alpha Phi mixer. "A crazy time."

I put my arm over his shoulder and guided him to the bar, where we picked four beers out of a bin filled with ice tended to by a woman in a gold string bikini, then walked back to our table in time to hear Natalya say, "I know you don't care for me, Fiona, but I could use a person like you."

"I don't get used," Fi said. She stood up abruptly. "Ever."

"Ladies," I said, stopping Natalya from whatever she was about to say. "I wanted to introduce you to an old friend just in town for a few days on business." I had my arm around Dixon and could feel him tensing. He knew this wasn't right. I just kept slurring right along. "This is Dixon Woods. He runs an opium operation out of Afghanistan, but he's also very active in the real estate market here, and he's employed by Longstreet Security, though I'm going to guess he's not telling them he's here this evening meeting with all of us."

"You're drunk," he said. "My name is—"

"No," I said, squeezing him tighter, letting spittle gather between my words. I kept his arms pressed against me so he couldn't reach for his gun, not that I thought he'd pull a gun in the middle of a crowded hotel.

But I would.

"Don't even bother. We're all friends. For instance, that's Natalya Choplyn. She's ex-KGB. You don't know it, Dixon, but you guys are now business partners. You should chat. Get to know each other."

I gave Fiona a glance, but she didn't need any signs from me. She already had two vials of tear gas in her hand. But she is much smarter than me, so she also had a glass of water in the other, and she promptly hurled the water on Natalya, soaking her.

At the same time, I slid my hand down Dixon's back, grasped his gun, and squeezed off a round through his pants, which sent him to the ground in a screaming heap, even though the bullet had buried itself in the ground. The scorch alone would put a man down, never mind the factor of surprise.

Not to be outdone, and probably because she'd been wanting to do it for years, Fiona grabbed Natalya by the throat and cracked a vial of tear gas right across her face and then flung another toward the bar, where the other Russians were now crouching from the gunfire.

Here's how tear gas works: It attacks wet spots on your body—tear and saliva ducts, mucous membranes, your tongue, your eyes, sweat glands—and creates an unbearable amount of pain and suffering, particularly if you get hit with it directly. If you happen to have your entire face covered with water, and you happen to be sweating, perhaps because you've just been involved in a multimillion-dollar deal with a spy who, in the process, has convicted you of economic espionage, it's likely to hurt quite a bit more.

Sam was supposed to set off his small explosions by now, but for some reason, as Fiona and I sprinted out toward the ocean, away from the toxic fumes of tear gas, nothing had happened yet.

The plan was for the Malibu lights to set off a series of small explosions that would sound like gunfire. He told me he was going to wire the solar fuses to a nichrome wire coated in solder, run them wire to wire, dip them in a dusting of gunpowder and surround them with match heads so that when the lights heated up—a reaction caused by their dip into darkness—he'd have a series of explosive squibs. Or just a really loud electrical match. He'd toss a blanket over them, and then, a few seconds later . . . things would go boom.

Sam promised me nothing would actually explode.

Sam promised me that it would just sound like gunfire.

Sam promised me that it would be enough to get Eddie Champagne, who he said he was going to lock in the bathroom, arrested without getting him killed.

I was thus more than a little surprised a few moments later, when Fiona and I were already lost in the crowd on the beach, when there was an enormous explosion that propelled most of the balcony of room 511 into the pool of the Hotel Oro, deck chairs, chaise longues, a lovely side table all airborne in fiery glory. Most of the crowd had already scattered, which was good, since little flaming bits of Malibu lights were raining down all around.

"That's not good," I said, but the truth was, it was better than I could have hoped, since it happened just as police and men wearing IRS windbreakers came storming into the pool area, followed, in due course, by James Dimon (snapping photos that were doubtlessly present in the moment) and scads of Longstreet men who found themselves armed to the teeth with no one to shoot or guard, since both Dixon Woods and Natalya Choplyn were right where we'd left them, on the ground, clawing at their own eyes from the tear gas, Fiona's BlackBerry still sitting on the table, loaded with all the documents anyone with a badge would need to piece together the workings of Natalya Choplyn and Dixon Woods, particularly the intimate details of how she was defrauding our mortgage system for the Russians.

I put my hand in Fiona's. "Nice work," I said.

"You surprised me with that gunshot," she said.

"I surprised myself," I said. "You know, you can blind someone by hitting them directly in the face with tear gas."

"Not permanently?"

"No," I said, "not permanently."

We moved through the thickening group of gawkers rushing to the hotel, our pace leisurely, just a nice couple out on the promenade, unconcerned with the sounds of sirens. We'd been seen, of course, but the people who really mattered—Natalya, Dixon and Eddie—didn't have any way to roll this toward us, so being relaxed wasn't just a pose.

My phone rang.

"How'd you like that bang?" Sam asked.

"It was supposed to be a little something less," I said.

"I must have gotten carried away with gunpowder," Sam said.

"Where's Eddie?"

"I'd say about five seconds from being cuffed for good. If you don't mind, while things are under way over here, I'm going to go get my car."

"Of course," I said.

"Tell Fi I expect some recourse," he said.

"Of course," I said again, though I'd let them fight that one out. I closed my phone and squeezed Fiona's hand. "Dinner?" I said to Fiona.

"Dessert?"

"No," I said. "Not tonight." But Fiona's hand was warm, the air was brilliant, and we'd won, so anything was possible.

Epilogue

What you can never tell about people in love is how they'll react when the person they profess to hate the most—usually the person who has done them the most wrong—is right in front of their face.

In Cricket O'Connor's case, that happened on the television the day after the explosion, when Eddie Champagne was a footnote to the local news reports of odd doings at the Hotel Oro. Apparently, on the same day a significant foreign spy was arrested for espionage, a low-level grifter accidentally blew up his hotel room. She was still at my mother's then, and I was there helping Cricket negotiate the transfer of some of her money back into the U.S. Legally.

When she saw Eddie on television, she went into the kitchen and spit into the sink.

"I still feel so stupid," she said. "I've lost so much."

"It will continue to eat at you," I said. "There's no cure for shame."

"Having some security again will help," she said. She meant her money.

"What are you going to do with it all?"

"I have to pay my mortgage," she said, and it looked painful for her to say. "And then after I do that, I'll sell the house, get what I can. Get out of Miami. Help who I can help from my son's unit along the way. See if it can't erase some of this."

"There will be others, too," I said.

"I know," she said.

"No," I said, "others who will come for your money."

"I know that, too," she said. On television, Eddie was shown being arraigned in court. "What will happen to Dixon?"

"Eddie," I said.

"Right. Eddie."

"I think he's going to prison. But he'll have company."

I'd see Cricket O'Connor a few times over the next couple of days, and though she offered me money for the work we did to help her, I declined it. It didn't stop Nate from offering to help her move when the time came. But over the next few weeks, I did watch with interest as White Rose Partners fell under federal indictment, as Eddie Champagne and a stunned, and always saddened-looking, Dixon Woods were tossed to the wolves, as Natalya Choplyn was hailed as one of the biggest counterintelligence arrests of the last ten years and then, like everything else, it all disappeared from the papers and, eventually, even I stopped thinking about it.

Then, two things happened on the same day.

First, Fiona finally received a very exciting e-mail. From Hank Fitch.

From: HFitch911@gmail.com
To: RubyRedKitty@yahoo.com
Subject: Up late in Miami?

   I saw your profile tonight for the first time and I
wanted you to know that you don't have to be
alone with your sorrow. There are many of us still
struggling with our grief but I've found that
being together makes it easier. A little bit about
me: I'm ex–Special Forces, which you've probably been told by every person online, but I play
it as it lays, Ruby. Would you be interested in
meeting for a drink sometime? I'm presently incar-
cerated, which isn't much of a selling point, but
I should be out soon and I'd love to meet up when
I'm out. I've attached a photo of myself on my
yacht so you can see I'm not some kind of serial
killer ☺

"Nice," I said. We were in my kitchen. I was eating yogurt after working out. Fi was gloating after rush-ing over to show me her good news. "You and your uncommon breasts should go visit him."

"Maybe I will," she said.

Second: My cell phone rang.

It was a blocked number, but I took it anyway. I'd already spoken to my mother once that day anyway and was due, in forty minutes, to drive her to her thousandth doctor appointment of the year.

"You should look up more often, Mr. Westen," the voice said. It was mechanical, run through voice-changing software. It might just be voice-recognition software, no human at all on the other end. Just a program.

"Maybe I should," I said.

"There is a plan," the voice said.

"Of course. There always is," I said, but the line was already dead.

I looked out my window and saw Sam pull up in his Cadillac, the windows repaired, the rims shining, the tires fully inflated. It was noon and yet when he got out of the car, he was holding a six-pack of something in one hand and a grocery bag in the other, and I actually saw him mumbling to himself, like he was practicing a presentation of some kind, getting his words right, as if he might need to convince someone to get involved in something.

Again.

burn notice
USA ORIGINAL SERIES
THURSDAYS

characters welcome.
usa network

burnnotice.usanetwork.com

BURN NOTICE SEASON 1 NOW AVAILABLE ON DVD

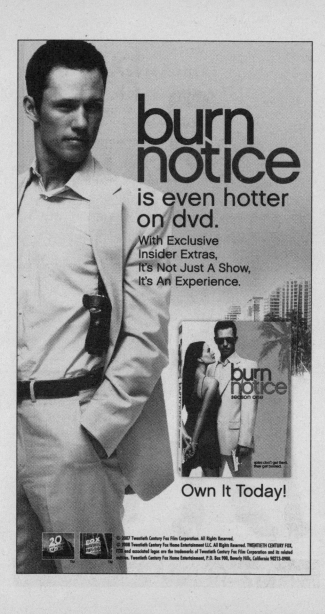

Obsessive.
Compulsive.
Detective.

MONK

The mystery series starring the
brilliant, beloved, and slightly
off-beat sleuth from the USA
Network's hit show!

Available wherever books are sold or at
penguin.com

CRIMINAL MINDS:
JUMP CUT

by
MAX ALLAN COLLINS

First in the brand-new series based on
the hit CBS television show!

The Behavioral Analysis Unit, an elite
team of FBI profilers, are tasked with
examining the nation's most twisted
criminal minds—anticipating their
next moves before they strike again...

<u>Also Available in the Series:</u>
Criminal Minds: Killer Profile
Criminal Minds: Finishing School

Available wherever books are sold or at
penguin.com